The
Final
Step

A NOVEL

ROB KAUFMAN

The Final Step

"Reading is like breathing in, writing is like breathing out."

~ Pam Allyn ~

PROLOGUE

This is the first and probably last time I'll write in this journal.

I'm only doing it because my shrink says it's supposed to lower stress and help with depression. I think that's bullshit. That's why I never did it until today. And the only reason I'm doing it today is because I'm scared. If this journaling thing really does work, it should help calm my nerves. I'd cross my fingers if I wasn't using them to write.

Okay, I'm not sure I'm doing this right, but here I go...

The first thing I'll say is: no one understands. Especially my family. They have no idea what it's like to wake up in the morning asking "why?" Why should I get out of bed? Why should I eat breakfast? Why should I keep breathing? Doing all that shit just gets me through another day so I can go back to sleep at night, wake up again tomorrow and ask "why?" a hundred times all over again.

My life is like a hamster on a wheel. Except my wheel has rungs covered in glue, maybe even melted taffy. It's messy and slows me down. Doesn't matter anyway because I'm not going anywhere.

They think pills are going to help. They think therapy is my ticket out. They think getting me to leave the house and see other people will bring me joy. Well, here's some news — pills only make my head dizzy, therapy just pisses me off and people, holy shit. Really? Just the thought of meeting or talking to strangers makes my stomach turn. People in general make me sick. Probably because they don't understand me either. And they don't even try.

If I'm sad, I'm sad. Can't I just be a sad person? Maybe my DNA doesn't have any happiness in it. That's not right or wrong. It's just the way it is.

It's that nature versus nurture thing my shrink talks about. I was born fat, ugly, sad and mad. That's nature. My father was almost as mean to me as the bullies at school. My sister was pretty and popular, my total opposite. She mostly ignored me after we grew up. And my mother just pitied me. Still does. That's nurture. Anyway, I'm still sad and mad, but now I'm skinny. No one, especially my piece of shit, who-cares-if-he's-dead-or-not father, can call me fat ever again.

I'm writing, but still don't understand how this journaling thing is supposed to help. Am I scribbling the right things? I'm feeling more depressed than when I started. But then, Doc said that could happen. He said letting the thoughts out, the ones I usually keep to myself, might bring other things to the surface. Things that might make me feel worse at first. And now that I feel like jumping off a bridge, that's probably a good thing because it means I'm doing it right. Right? I'm so fucking confused.

I almost just gave up on this writing thing, but I'll force myself to continue because I have a bad feeling. I know this might sound crazy, but I think my family is trying to get rid of me. Maybe I went too far. Or maybe they're just afraid that the fantasy of their perfect family will crumble. I am so alone.

"It's all about family. Family staying together is our number one priority." That's all my sister ever says. But she's talking about her family. Her little picture-perfect family. A family I'm not a part of.

One or all of them is after me. I know it. I can feel it, way down deep in that place my shrink says I keep my unused intuition.

My mother is sick of me. Tired of me living in her house, watching over me and listening to my complaints. Without me around, maybe she could live a normal life. At least that's what she probably thinks. Ha! Her demons are worse than mine and she doesn't even know it. Removing me from her life won't change that, but the facts she can't confront won't stop her from trying. Is she going to poison my food? Smother me in the middle of the night with a pillow? Would a mother really kill her own kid?

Holy shit. I really do sound crazy, like I'm talking to someone else, but I'm talking to myself. Right?

Carrie hates me, too. With everything that's happened, I can tell she wishes I didn't exist. I know she's always felt that way, even growing up, but now it's worse. My sister's house of cards is falling apart and she's not sure how to keep it standing. It would probably be a lot easier to keep her family's flawless reputation if I wasn't around. How would she get rid of me? Would she hire someone? She's got enough money, that's for sure. How would he do it? A knife? A gun? Strangle me?

Should I tell the cops? Yeah, right. They'd call me crazy. Just like everyone else does.

Shit.

Andrew hates me most of all. I get it. He actually always hated me. And now — holy crap, I can't even write about what's going on 'cause my hands would shake too much. If anyone wants me off this planet, it's him. He's probably the only one who would do it with his bare hands, too, after what I did. But if he killed me, Jack would grow up with a father in prison. Would he do that to his only child?

I just read this over from the beginning and think everyone might be right. I really think I could be nuts. Now I know why the shrink says to write everything down and then shred it. It's kind of like letting out your feelings, thoughts, craziness and shit, then taking all that shit and dumping it out like it never existed. Maybe throwing it all away will help get rid of it from my brain, help me stop thinking about it and stop worrying that someone is going to kill me.

If I am crazy and everything I wrote is paranoid garbage, at least I got it off my chest. And maybe it will disappear. If what I wrote isn't psycho trash and someone really is gonna murder me, then at least I won't have to wake up to another day of asking the question "why?" a thousand times.

My killer will have taken care of that for me.

CHAPTER ONE

Carrie had rehearsed the words in her mind all day, preparing herself for her husband's reaction. But practice didn't make the prospect of saying them out loud any easier. She took a deep breath, mustered her courage, and spoke.

"Ellen's coming for a visit." She set the plate of reheated lasagna on the table in front of him.

Across from her, Jack remained engrossed in his phone, equally unaware of the cooling meal before him and the conversation breaking out between his parents. Andrew, on the other hand, nearly choked on the Johnnie Walker he had been savoring.

He swallowed hard as his whisky glass slammed onto the handcrafted dining table.

"Wait...why?" He regained control of his throat and mouth, but couldn't hide his annoyance, not when it came to Ellen. "Why is she coming here?"

"Because she's my younger sister and I haven't seen her in

almost a year. If you remember, we spent the holidays with *your* family." Carrie sat down without meeting his eyes.

With the neat placement of a white napkin on her lap, she attempted to signal the end of their conversation. She speared a cherry tomato from her salad but glanced at her son before taking a bite. "Jack...what did we talk about regarding phones at dinnertime?"

He swiped his fingers across the keyboard, quickly finishing a text before placing his phone on the table.

"She's not right in the head, Carrie," Andrew said, taking another sip of whisky. "You know that. And she drinks too much. I don't like her hanging around Jack. She's a bad influence."

Carrie picked the tomato from her fork with her front teeth, chewing slowly. Fatigue and frustration washed over her, accumulated from a long day of work, preparing dinner and trying to get ready for this confrontation with Andrew. No matter how many times they'd discussed or fought about her sister, he just couldn't understand her relationship with Ellen. It was complicated and personal, a strange bond held together for decades by threads of obligation, guilt, and pity, a connection only she and her sister understood, but never spoke about.

"Do I complain when your brothers come to visit?" she asked, stepping directly into the line of fire.

"Yeah," Andrew replied. "You do."

Carrie sighed. "Well, that's because they're pretentious and callous," she blurted, her anger and exhaustion slipping through. "The two of them act like they're God's gift to the world, and to be perfectly honest —"

"Don't be," Andrew huffed, looking at Jack. "This really isn't the time or place." He shifted his attention back to Carrie. "I'll say it again. She's not a good influence."

Carrie dropped her fork onto the plate, causing a loud clank that made Jack flinch. "He knows right from wrong. He knows his Aunt Ellen and the struggles she has. He won't become an alcoholic because a woman he sees three times a year drinks too much."

"I'm sorry, honey," she said to their son, who was absentmindedly pushing lumps of ricotta cheese off his lasagna. "I didn't mean to talk about you as if you weren't here."

Jack shrugged. "No worries."

His response to everything.

"The woman is thirty-nine, Carrie, and she can't even hold down a job bagging groceries. How hard is it to pack a cereal box properly or keep the eggs on top? Or was it the stolen pack of gum that got her fired last time?"

Carrie's stomach churned, wiping out her appetite... and her patience.

"I thought you said this wasn't the time or place." Her voice cracked as it got louder, her anger swelling.

"It isn't," Andrew agreed. "My bad."

Your bad is right. "And just so you know, Mom says she's on a new med that seems to be helping. She's more alert and energetic. Supposedly, her attitude is better too. She's not as depressed."

"Honey..." Andrew's affection for her showed in his obvious effort to keep his tone gentle. "Again, is this the time and place?"

Carrie shrugged. *Oh my God, I'm just like Jack.*

"It's not," she agreed. "But I *do* know that if she looked different, you'd like her more. It's her appearance that makes her visits unbearable, right?"

3

This time Andrew dropped his fork. "Are you seriously asking me if I'd like your sister more if she looked like Miss America? That it wouldn't matter that she drinks like a sot, lives in pajama bottoms, curses like a sailor, can't keep a job, and lives with her mother at thirty-nine years old?" He took a swig of whisky and feigned laughter. "Are you kidding me?"

She cast a glance in Jack's direction. He looked perplexed — was he growing anxious? Suppressing the tingle of frustration surging through her body, she mustered a false smile.

As her eyes locked with his, memories of his past struggles flashed through her mind, catapulting her back five years.

After performing a battery of medical tests, their primary physician sent them to Dr. Robert Barnes, a well-known psychiatrist whose office was a stone's throw from theirs, just across the border between Darien and Stamford. Not even fifteen minutes after Jack went in, the doctor's office door creaked open and he invited Carrie and Andrew to join them. By the time they settled in the chairs facing his desk, his fingers were already dancing across the keyboard.

"Now, what I'm going to do is prescribe Klonopin —"

"Dr. Barnes," Carrie interjected, "I was hoping we could explore other avenues." She turned to Jack. He shuffled in his chair, clasping his fingers and clenching his hands. Carrie cursed herself. She should have had Jack wait outside. *Too late now.* "I was thinking we'd start with things like stress reduction, biofeedback, something more...natural. We don't want to rely on medications right away. They have side effects, especially for a young boy."

His gaze flickered, barely acknowledging her before returning to the computer screen. How dare he? His dismissive attitude intensified Carrie's anger into an inferno. She rose from her seat. Andrew reached out, attempting to grab her hand, but she shrugged off his touch.

"No," Carrie said. "Jack won't be taking Klonopin. And I find it troubling, doctor, that you can't spare a moment to look at us when discussing our son. Jack is not a test subject for your clinical trials." Taking Jack's hand, she lifted him from the chair, her hold firm but gentle. "I won't have a son dependent on medication for the rest of his life. We're done here!" she declared and led him out of the room, deaf to the protests trailing in their wake.

Days turned into weeks as Carrie delved into her research, seeking an alternative path to Jack's healing. She searched relentlessly until she found Dr. Stanton, who shared her belief in non-prescription treatments like cognitive behavior therapy, hypnosis, and biofeedback. She and Andrew met with the psychologist for over an hour, then made a pact to work with Dr. Stanton for two to three months on nighttime safety and identifying triggers. If there was no progress, they'd seek another psychiatrist and consider medication. But she'd be damned if they returned to that self-absorbed Dr. Barnes.

One night, after putting Jack to bed, Andrew and Carrie went into the study downstairs to enjoy a little time together. He tended to the fire, coaxing the embers to life, and sat in the beige button-tufted wingback chair next to Carrie's. He watched the smoke get sucked up by the flue as Carrie cradled her tablet and opened a PowerPoint presentation from a meeting she'd missed that day.

"Do you think he has what Ellen has?"

Carrie dropped the tablet on her lap. It struck her thighs

with a flopping sound, but that didn't smart half as badly as the bruise of his veiled accusation. "And what exactly does Ellen have?" she asked.

"I meant...well...you know. He might have a mental illness or disorder or...something."

Carrie's fingers drummed on the tablet's leather case, her frustration mounting. Her love for Andrew had weathered the test of time, but his black-and-white perspective, his refusal to see the shades of gray, was incredibly frustrating. What is he saying now? Jack can either be "normal" or mentally ill? There's no middle ground — no possibility their son's problems might be temporary and fixable?

She'd learned how to compartmentalize their other marital problems, but this close-mindedness, this tunnel vision he couldn't seem to free himself from, was suffocating. She leaned forward, and said with both weariness and determination, "Andrew, we've had this conversation countless times. Ellen's issues stem from childhood trauma and her longstanding battle with depression. Jack is different, you heard Dr. Stanton. He's hypervigilant, in a constant state of fight-or-flight. It's a symptom, not a disorder."

"But a symptom of *what?*" Andrew asked. "What has happened in the boy's life that would make him so nervous and worried?"

"I don't know," she said. She bit her bottom lip in an attempt to keep the peace, but the words slipped out before she had a chance to stop them. "Why do *you* have bouts of depression? What happened in *your* life that would have you enjoying life one minute and keeping silent and isolated the next?"

Andrew turned to the fire. The flames' reflection danced in his eyes as she waited for him to respond. She knew he'd never answer truthfully, if at all. She also knew it was better that way. The only reason she'd asked the question in the first place was so he'd realize the foolishness of his own question.

"Anxiety and stress, I think," she said, cutting through the uncomfortable silence. "It runs in our family and Jack was unlucky enough to get the gene."

Andrew kept his eyes on the fire, its glow casting moving shadows across his face.

"It doesn't make sense. He comes from a loving home where there's basically no stress. If you ask me, it's a little *too* quiet around here." She didn't return his forced smile. "He's the star of every school play, so he definitely doesn't have stage fright. He's got an amazing voice that he uses at rehearsal every day, which proves he's not scared to sing or speak in public. He gets good grades without having to study too hard. He's got a group of friends who he —"

"Andrew," Carrie said, her stomach tightening around the pit at its center, "you're preaching to the choir. I know about Jack's life. I know what he does and what he doesn't do." She squeezed the hard vinyl cover of her tablet to help restrain herself from raising the topic of his depression again. "You need to understand — none of that matters. From the research I've done, some people are just born with a highly sensitive nervous system that can lead to things like panic attacks and night terrors. It's the whole nature versus nurture thing. This might just be his nature and it's up to us to help him cope and also... fingers crossed...help him get rid of them."

To Andrew's surprise and Carrie's delight, her vigilance and crossed fingers paid off. Guided by Dr. Stanton and the support of a group of parents facing similar challenges, they fought, tooth and nail, to ease Jack's nighttime fears, and in time, their battle was won.

Nearly three years had passed since his last episode, and she refused to let a squabble over Ellen's visit unravel their hard-fought progress. Dealing with distress and anxiety outside this house was hard enough. The last thing Jack needed was tension between his parents adding to the mix. "There's no need for you to sit and listen to this, honey," she said to Jack. "Take your dinner to your room if you'd like."

He grabbed his plate, his lips curled in a half-smile. Halfway to the staircase, he stopped and turned back. "Texting allowed?"

Carrie chuckled, shaking her head. "Yes, sweetheart."

Once their son's door closed, Carrie locked eyes with Andrew. Waiting for him to speak first would be futile. Even after seventeen years, it was still a mystery why he only spoke his mind around others and not when they were alone. She'd broached the subject numerous times, but he'd push it aside like all the other uncomfortable topics he'd become so adept at avoiding.

"Andrew, it's just one weekend," she said. "She'll get here on Friday and we'll put her back on the train on Sunday. It'll give my mom a break and maybe I can talk with her and see where her head is at. She might actually be better, like Mom said. Let's just see how it goes and take it from there. You may never want to see her again or you may like her enough to want her to visit again next weekend."

She smiled, his response on the tip of her own tongue even as he said, with a wry smile tugging at his lips, "Not likely."

Carrie chuckled, warmth driving away the chill that had coursed through her body just moments before. She stood, walked behind his chair and kissed his left earlobe. When he looked up at her, she bent over further to cover his mouth with hers.

After a passionate kiss, he shook his head and grinned. "You have a way with words."

A pang from deep inside her groin provided a burst of energy she hadn't been able to muster all day. "I have a way with more than just words," she quipped back. She laughed at herself, realizing how she'd also become adept at avoiding awkward topics.

Andrew kept smiling, seemingly not picking up on the rueful note in her laugh. He rose from his chair, lifted their plates from the table and walked into the kitchen, placing both nearly full dishes on the island countertop. She watched his butt flex in his sleek trousers and grinned as her husband said,

"Let's get these dishes done and find out."

Carrie walked into Jack's bedroom, where he sat with ankles crossed up on his desk, pods deep in his ears and thumbs tapping on his phone so quickly they were a blur. She leaned down and placed a kiss on the top of his head.

Jack removed his earbuds and looked up at her, a spark of curiosity in his eyes.

"I came in to say goodnight. We're going to bed early tonight. Long day."

"Okay," he said, but the left side of his upper lip was crimped.

"What is it? I see that look on your face."

Jack pursed his lips. "What's wrong with Aunt Ellen?"

"What do you mean?" Carrie sat on the edge of his desk. "Nothing's wrong with Aunt Ellen."

"Then why doesn't Dad like her? And why does he think she's a bad influence on me? I mean, yeah, she's a little weird and drinks, but she's always been nice to me."

She leaned forward and tousled his thick waves of chocolate-brown hair. "It's not that Dad doesn't like her. There are just some things he wishes she did differently."

"You mean like how Tom Watson looks like an idiot with his mohawk? Or how Macy Franco talks so loud that Mrs. Lane has to tell her to lower the volume every time she answers a question?"

Carrie laughed softly. "Yes," she said. "Like that. Just because you don't like the way Tom's hair looks or how loud Macy speaks, doesn't mean they're not good people, does it?"

Jack shrugged. "I guess not. Do you think Dad doesn't like her because she's so skinny?"

Carrie closed her eyes, taking a moment to compose herself. She thought about Andrew waiting for her in the bedroom down the hall and didn't want a conversation about Ellen to dampen the flame of her desire for him. She loved her husband, truly, but lust was rarer, unpredictable, and she wanted to enjoy it when she felt it, like tonight.

"No, Jack. It's not because she's skinny."

"Is it because she looks funny?" Jack pressed on.

"What do you mean, 'looks funny'?"

He dropped his eyes to his phone, raised them again, then blurted out, "Well, not really funny. Just...I don't know...ugly."

"Jack! Why would you say something like that?"

"Because you asked me!"

The vision of a ten-year-old Ellen standing naked in front of the bedroom mirror, pinching the skin under her arms, brought Carrie to tears. Peeking in from the slightly ajar bathroom door she saw the revulsion in her sister's eyes, her drooping mouth, the corners of which came close to reaching her chin. And her eyes... the hurt and welling tears as she crossed her arms over her small breasts in an attempt to hide them. The weight of her self-judgment, along with that of her father and teenagers devoid of compassion or empathy, had scarred her in ways Carrie knew she, herself, would never understand.

Standing up, she cradled Jack's chin, urging him to meet her eyes.

"Aunt Ellen is not ugly and she does not look funny," she said firmly. "She is who she is like I am who I am and you are who you are. Just because someone doesn't look like you think they should, doesn't make them ugly."

He turned to his phone and started putting his ear pods back in. "Well, Dad says she's ugly."

Before he pushed the second pod inside, Carrie pulled lightly on his earlobe. "Oh, he does, does he? I'll have to have a little talk with your dad. In the meantime, don't stay up too late." She planted another kiss on his forehead before going out. She closed the door behind her, then leaned against it, trying to regain control of her emotions and steady her racing heart.

In their bedroom, Carrie found Andrew naked and smirking. The white sheet barely covered his groin, and the shadows of his abdominal muscles hinted at his earlier exercise routine. *Show-off.*

As she moved toward the king-size bed, she removed her top, revealing the Journelle lace bra that cradled her ample breasts — breasts that Andrew caressed and used with a sense of entitlement, often in ways she didn't care for, but surrendered to so he'd be able to climax with little effort. Undoing the belt of her black print midi skirt, she let it fall to the floor, leaving her standing in front of him in nothing but her bra and panties. Leaning over the edge of the bed, she exposed her cleavage and hard nipples to Andrew's gaze.

Andrew's eyes widened, his mouth opening to take in a breath. His legs shifted beneath the covers revealing his anticipation.

"So Ellen is ugly?" she asked, her voice laced with a combination of seduction and accusation.

Andrew's flirtatious expression twisted into confusion. Carrie couldn't quite explain why, but the sight of his bewildered face brought her more satisfaction than any physical pleasure could.

"What are you talking about?" he stuttered.

She stood and shook her head slightly, letting her silky hair cascade across her back and shoulders. She knew the sight excited him. Made him want her.

Softly, she told him, "Jack said he heard you say she was ugly."

"I don't think I ever used that word. I really don't —"

"He used the word 'ugly,' Andrew. He wouldn't say that unless he heard it from you. You know how he hangs on your every word." Carrie frowned, the atmosphere of desire thickening into a more bitter tension. "That's just plain mean. You know that, right?"

Andrew reached out. "Let me make it up to you." His smile was hesitant at first, trembling on his lips, but as he looked at her body, it became amorous.

With a hiss, she pulled her hair back, unhooked her bra and strode into the bathroom.

"Make it up to yourself," she spat before slamming the door shut and drowning out his response with a turn of the shower faucet.

CHAPTER TWO

E llen's bedroom window shade was closed, leaving only the ceiling light above her head to illuminate her face. She looked at herself in the mirror and traced the circles under her eyes with her middle finger, hoping shadows were responsible for the skeletal figure staring back at her.

When she ran all her fingers through her brittle hair, pulling at the gray wisps among the sienna-colored strands, her short fingernails caught on the split ends. She tried to remove a flake of skin from her bottom lip with her teeth. That didn't work. The skin peeled further until it hung from her mouth. Irritated, she gripped it between her thumb and index finger, then tore it off with a soft exclamation of pain.

"Ow, shit." She pulled the tube of Chapstick from the pocket of her jeans and smeared it across her lips. *Driest fucking skin in the world. Matches my personality...my life.*

Her gaze remained fixed on the mirror as she lifted the oversized black V-neck tee that hung on her like a drenched towel. She examined her stomach by pinching the skin above her jeans, but found it too taut to squeeze. The prominence of her rib cage through her thin skin became visible as she lifted her shirt higher, revealing breasts so flat they were barely discernible. With an involuntary shudder, she let her shirt fall and then collapsed onto the bed, staring at the shadows cast by the small protrusions on the stippled ceiling.

Skin and bones. I'm skin and bones. Her reflection both disgusted her and filled her with a sense of pride. *He can't call me fat now.*

It had been almost twenty-two years since her mother finally threw her father out.

He came home in his usual drunken state, plopping down on the living room sofa without a care in the world, covered from shirt to boots in splattered stain and paint from the job site. Did he even consider that the paint on his shirt would smear all over the couch? Or that the stench of wood stain from his jeans would remain in the cushions for days?

Ellen and Carrie watched TV from the floor, lying on their stomachs in their flannel nightshirts, their hands propping up their heads. They were engrossed in an episode of *I Love Lucy* when the drunk lump on the couch leaned over and started stroking Carrie's hair. The terror in her sister's eyes sent electric jolts down Ellen's spine. She searched for her mother, unsure of what to do. Did it matter? Her mother never did anything anyway. His physical and verbal abuse hung in the air day and night, diminishing only during those rare occasions he'd be missing for days at a time. But no one really cared. His absence brought freedom from the tension. They'd smile more. Laugh louder. Know what it felt like to be a family, even if it was only the three of them.

Carrie pulled away from the stroking hand and ran to the top of the stairs.

"What's up with Miss Pretty girl?" their father slurred. "A dad can't touch his own daughter's hair?"

Ellen sat up without uttering a word, her stomach tied in knots of fear. Should she stay or go to Carrie, who sat watching them from the top step?

"What's up with you?" he asked, sinking back into the sofa cushions. "Ya know, you should start tak- takin' lessons from your sister. Lose some fucking weight, girl. G-get a figure like hers. I mean, Jesus, do something to yourself, 'cau-cause that face ain't getting you nowhere. If I was you —"

"Ben!" their mom shouted from the kitchen. "Shut your goddamn mouth this second!"

She stood under the archway between the rooms, holding a wet plaid dishtowel in one hand and a rolling pin in the other. There was something different in her mother's tone that night, something that signaled a departure from their usual shouting matches. Another cold jolt sparked down Ellen's spine.

"Ahhh, Michelle. Ca-calm your jets. I'm just talking to the girl. She's gotta know — know the truth sometime. Sh-she picked the short straw when it came to looks and br-brains. Must take after *your* side of the family."

Michelle gave Ellen a quick glance. "Go upstairs," she commanded. "Now." Then she turned to the man on the couch and stared him down, her eyes on fire.

Ellen jumped up, her floral-patterned nightshirt barely covering her pudgy thighs. She felt her father's look slide over them like slime. Carrie motioned for her to sit beside her on the top step. Together they peered through the wooden banisters.

Ellen's heart felt like it was pinched between two giant fingers. She felt scared and almost excited.

"I want you out of here," Michelle said, her voice loud and unsteady. "I'm sick of you and your disgusting drunken behavior. I don't trust you and don't want you near Carrie or Ellen. Now get out!"

"I don't know what the hell you're talking about. Now give me that-that — whatever that thing is and get back in the kitchen where you belong."

"Out!" she yelled. "I said get out! I'm done with this shit and I'm done with you! If you don't leave on your own, I'll make you leave!"

"Hey," Ben said, attempting to sit up straight. "Hey, who the fu —" Michelle raised the rolling pin until she was holding it next to her face. "Wh-wh-what? You gonna hit me with that? Go ahead. Try it. Wa-watch what happens when —"

"N-no, Ben." She took a deep breath, and when she spoke again, her voice was softer and steadier. "I'm not going to hit you with it." She slammed the rolling pin against her other hand, so hard the dishtowel half wrapped around it. "I'm going to hit *me* with it."

Ellen and Carrie looked at each other. What was Mom thinking? The pinching fingers in Ellen's chest tightened. Her sister reached for her hand.

"What are yo-you talking about, you stupid —"

"I'm talking about hitting myself in the face with this rolling pin." Her voice grew louder again, but still steady, as if she'd practiced saying this. "Until my face is bleeding and my eyes swell shut. Then I'm going to call the cops and tell them my husband beat me." She walked over to him and held the rolling pin above his head. "I'll tell them you tried to kill me and they'll throw you in prison for years."

Ben ran his fingers through his greasy black hair and laughed, cackling so loud, the pinch in Ellen's heart crawled up into her throat, almost choking her. Carrie tightened her grip on Ellen's hand.

"You wouldn't do that. Id-idiot. You're too chicken. And who would pay for this house? Your food?" He turned to the staircase, where Ellen and Carrie glared at him. "And those two. Who's gonna take care of them?" Eyeing the rolling pin, he attempted to stand. "You ain't got it in you. Now gimme that thing and go finish washing some dishes or something."

The sound of the blow echoed through the house. Ellen felt paralyzed, unable to move any part of her body other than her head and eyes. Downstairs, their mom shuffled her feet to regain her balance as she lowered the rolling pin. Her face was red, an angry sunburn look spreading from the cheek she'd hit, the left one, and her shoulders heaved as she took a deep, trembling breath. Their father, still sitting on the sofa, leaned forward.

"Holy shit, I can't believe you just did that!" He put his hands on his knees. The muscles in his arms bulged as he tried to push himself to standing. It didn't work. He fell back onto the cushions. "You better cut that shit out or —"

"Or what?" Michelle yelled. Blood dripped from a gash the rolling pin had opened on her cheekbone. "Are you going to hit me? Go ahead. I'll just add it to the list when the cops get here." She pointed toward Carrie and Ellen. "I have witnesses right there. So go ahead, punch me!"

Carrie glanced at Ellen. Their hands, still holding each other, trembled. She tried to rise from the step, but Ellen swiftly pulled her back down.

"I think we should go down there," Carrie whispered. "What if she keeps hurting herself?"

Ellen couldn't figure out why, but something about the scene unfolding below eased the pressure in her stomach and throat. A strange calmness washed over her, and something more: a twisted delight at the fact that the two people who brought her into this world to suffer were about to suffer, too. She imagined her mother battered and bloodied, inflicting harm on herself until she could barely stand. And her father reduced to a pitiful existence, wandering the streets or locked up in jail without a family or ounce of sympathy from anyone. What better way for a night to end?

"No," she said to her sister. "Mom's not going to kill herself with that rolling pin and Dad's a coward. Once he can stand up, he'll leave and never come back. And don't you *want* that?" Carrie looked at her but didn't answer. "I know you do. I know what he's tried to do to you. And Mom knows, too. I just can't believe it took her this long to do something about it."

"Michelle, if you don't put that fucking thing down —"

This time she struck her right cheekbone with the handle of the rolling pin.

It took a few seconds longer for her swaying to stabilize. Once it did, she looked him dead in the eyes.

"What are you waiting for, *dear?* Aren't you going to hit me? I'm waiting!"

Michelle shoved her face toward him, eyes wide. Nothing. She waited a few more seconds. Still, nothing.

Ben shook his head and covered his face with his hands. Ellen watched him like a character in a thriller. *What is he going to do?* she wondered as if she were guessing about an actor in a movie. *What will be his next move?*

After what felt like an eternity, he grasped the arm of the couch, using it to lift himself to his feet. He gathered what little sobered balance he could muster and dragged himself toward the front door, rocking ever so slightly. After grabbing the doorknob, he paused and turned to shoot Michelle a scowl that pierced Ellen's heart and left her numb.

"You are one crazy bitch," he spat. Then, his gaze shifted to Carrie and Ellen, huddled at the top of the staircase. "And you two, Jesus Christ. One's gonna be a whore and the other a stupid pig in a loony bin."

Before he could leave on that poisonous note, Michelle hurled the rolling pin at him. One handle struck him in the ribcage, eliciting a pained yelp.

She rushed toward him, but he yanked the door, got through and slammed it shut. Ellen half expected her mother to chase after him — even looked forward to it. Instead she locked the door behind him, leaning against it for support.

Carrie raced down the stairs and Ellen followed. By the time they reached her, Michelle was on her knees, arms outstretched, her eyes swollen and bloodstained streaks marking her cheeks and neck.

"It's just us now, girls, a whole new life," she whispered as they embraced her tightly. "A better life. I promise."

Carrie wept as Ellen stared at the closed door behind her mother. Seven words echoed inside her head: *a stupid pig in a loony bin.*

Her phone, lying on her bed, rang, startling Ellen into a flinch. She picked it up and saw Carrie's number displayed on the screen. Not in the mood for a conversation, she contemplated ignoring the call and letting it go to voicemail.

However, she knew she would never be in the mood to talk. With a sigh, she tapped the green icon and closed her eyes.

"Hey," she said.

"Hey back!" Carrie's voice chimed, full of cheerfulness and vivacity.

Ugh. Why is she always so happy?

"What's up?"

"Just checking to make sure you're still coming on Friday and to see what time your train arrives."

Ellen sat up, scooted off the bed and walked to the window. She pulled up the shade and scanned the street below. As usual, it was empty. Sure, it was the middle of the day, but this entire town was like a morgue. *Give me a stray cat, a runaway dog, a squirrel running up that giant elm.* But there was no sign of life, and an unexpected sense of loneliness washed over her. Did she really want to fill that void with Carrie and her picture-perfect family? Unfortunately, she'd made a promise to both Carrie and their mother, and since she had nothing else to do, why not keep it?

She cleared her throat with a small cough. "Yeah, I'll be there. I think the train gets in about four-thirty." She heard voices in the background. "You at work?"

"Yes, sorry. Busy day, as usual."

Ellen rolled her eyes, silently mocking the remark.

"So you'll be here around four-thirty, you said?" her sister asked.

"Yeah, I messed up and made plans with Maria to hang out. I just need to cancel with her, and then I'm good to go."

"Oh, you still see Maria?"

"Yeah, we hang out every once in a while," she lied. In truth, she hadn't spoken to her childhood friend in over three years, since the heated argument in which Maria called her an agoraphobe. Ellen had tried explaining the difference between agoraphobia and her mere distaste for people. But the quarrel escalated to the point of her calling Maria a "shit for brains." Maria retaliated with an accusation that she hated people because they thought she was so ugly. It took every ounce of self-restraint for Ellen not to slap her only friend across the face. Instead, she kicked Maria out of the house and ignored her subsequent voicemails and texts. She didn't care that *all* of her days and nights would now be spent alone. It was plain and simple, she wasn't agoraphobic and Maria was a bitch. Screw Maria and screw their friendship.

"It's okay," she told Carrie. "I haven't seen you guys in forever. She'll understand."

"Perfect. Jack's really looking forward to it. Fortunately, he doesn't have a rehearsal this weekend, so you can spend some quality time with him. He's in his school's production of *West Side Story*. He's playing Tony."

Of course he is.

Maybe Carrie sensed something from her, because she added, "You can see how you feel while you're here. No pressure to do anything. We'll just hang out, catch up, and have some fun."

Yeah, fun.

"Okay," Ellen said. She fought the urge to ask, but couldn't help herself. "What about Andrew? Is he also looking forward to my visit?"

She already knew the answer. The man despised *her* almost as much as she did him.

After a few seconds of silence, Carrie forced out a half-hearted chuckle. "You know Andrew. Always busy with work and trying to get new clients. I'm not sure if he looks forward to anything."

Oh, she's good.

"I have to go now." The background voices grew louder. "But I'll be sure to be at the Darien station at four-thirty on Friday. See you then, okay?

Before Ellen had the time to respond, the line went silent.

"Okay," she muttered to the empty air. "See you then."

Great. A weekend with people. I can't wait.

She tossed her phone onto the bed and caught sight of the Fluoxetine bottle on her nightstand.

"Shit!" she moaned, smacking her forehead. She'd forgotten to take her meds again, and if her mother found out, another argument would surely follow. Ellen made her way to the pill bottle, unscrewed the cap, and shook a single green and white capsule into her palm. Why did her mother and doctor insist on her taking these meds? Was she any happier now than she was two months ago when she started them? No. So why bother?

Her mother would disagree.

"I am who I am," Ellen said during a recent dinner with Michelle. "If I'm sad, I'm sad. Pills won't magically make me happy if life sucks."

"That's true," her mother acknowledged. "You're right. But it's not so much that you're sad. Your sadness turns to anger, which makes you mean. Then you take it out on other people. And since you...well...because you don't go out much, those other people are *me*. I think the Fluoxetine has kept that anger under control better than anything else you've tried."

Ellen used her fork to push the peas around her plate in the shape of a smiley face.

"I know you're not happy, Ellen. And honestly, I don't know

anyone in this world who's *always* happy. But Dr. Blout said it could take a few months for the pills to work. Right now, I truly believe you're less angry than before. Maybe, in a few more weeks, a glimmer of happiness might even creep in...at least from time to time. Promise me you'll keep taking the medication. At least for another month or two?"

Ellen shook her head, speared two peas with her fork and let them fall on her tongue one at a time.

"I promise," she said.

She took the pill from her hand, tossed it back into the bottle, then rushed out of her bedroom and down the stairs to the liquor cabinet. With only a half hour left until her mother returned from her tutoring session, she needed a quick shot or two to get through the rest of the day. Her next opportunity for alcohol would be the small glass of wine her mother allowed with dinner, but it did little to quell her restless thoughts.

On her knees in front of the cabinet, she downed two shots of Jack Daniel's, then wiped her mouth on her arm. As the warmth soaked through her, she heard her mother's voice echoing somewhere in the dark recesses of her mind: *"And promise me you won't sneak alcohol while I'm not home, okay?"*

She took one more shot and returned the bottle back to its place inside the cabinet.

"I promise," she replied to the voice inside her head.

Promises, promises.

CHAPTER THREE

As she stepped into the meeting room in the church basement, the soft chatter from the parent support group members along with the space's warm and inviting atmosphere enveloped Michelle. The soft lighting from the wall sconces cast a comforting glow that embraced the room and helped soothe her unexplainable anxiety. Maybe it was because she had to be there in the first place that made her tense. Or possibly it was her fear of public speaking that made her uncomfortable. Whatever it was, she hadn't yet been able to figure it out. Maybe this would be the session that would help her find the answer. She could only hope. Then again, she'd had the same hope before every other session leading up to today, so her optimism flag wasn't really flying at full mast.

This group offered support for parents dealing with the challenges of raising troubled children. Embarrassed that her daughter was thirty-nine years old, while the other parents were struggling with children at least fifteen years younger, Michelle shared little, other than her name and that she had a "problem daughter." She spent most of her time listening and absorbing as much information as she could to help herself cope with Ellen and her special needs.

Michelle sat in one of the comfortably cushioned chairs in the circle, placed her pocketbook on her lap and glanced around the room, hoping to absorb more of its peace. The walls, painted in soothing blues and gentle earth tones, were adorned with uplifting artwork and motivational quotes. Reading *"Gratitude Springs From The Soul"* beneath an image of sprouting sunflowers, Michelle could almost believe it this time. She felt the tension in her shoulders loosen.

At the front of the room, a large flip chart was used to share information, brainstorm ideas, document strategies, or plan solutions for their children's challenges. The bulletin board behind it also displayed lists of community resources, helpful contacts, and upcoming events. In one corner of the room, a small bookshelf held a collection of relevant literature and self-help resources. Michelle had checked out some of the books on parenting techniques, mental health, and communication skills. But she couldn't say for certain whether they'd helped.

If they did, she thought, *I wouldn't have to be here right now.*

Other parents had gathered around the corner table for coffee, tea, and snacks. Healthy snacks, because Tom, the leader of the group, encouraged them to find the right nourishment for both the body and the spirit. Their murmurs drifted to Michelle, soft with compassion and heavy with understanding. This was a sanctuary where people came together, listened to one another, and found some of the solace they sought in knowing they weren't alone in their struggles.

What was wrong with her that she couldn't feel the same? Why was standing around a table with a cup of tea and a pleasant expression not in her cards? Maybe *she* was the reason Ellen was like she was. The girl had a mother who couldn't fit in anywhere. Not even in a place as inviting and compassionate as this. She was different than all the other people in the room... or was she?

After what felt like an interminable half hour of listening to the parents who always took the lead, Michelle found Tom's eyes fixed on her. Her heart skipped a beat and an alarming sense of anticipation washed over her. Was he going to call on her to speak?

"Michelle?" He always used their first names when he spoke, building a sense of familiarity that seemed to comfort other parents, but felt almost too intimate to her.

She nodded, beads of perspiration forming on the back of her neck.

"I don't want to pressure you, but it's been a while since we heard from you. Do you have anything to share about your daughter?"

God, how she wanted to be a part of the conversation, to release her pent-up frustrations and maybe even find reason to hope when it came to dealing with her daughter's issues. But she thought of telling them the full truth — how old Ellen was, how long this battle had raged without victory, how defeated she'd let herself be by it — and her lips pursed as she slowly shook her head.

"We're all in this together," Tom reassured her. "There is absolutely nothing to be embarrassed about. May I ask how old your daughter is?"

She thought about lying, but realized that would make the

reason she was there in the first place pointless. *Really*, she told herself, *you're here for help. Get some!*

Unable to stop the nerves from leading her to pick at the strap of her handbag, she muttered, "Thirty-nine."

The gasps and stifled chokes she expected to hear never came. She took a deep breath and let it out slowly. The tension she'd felt every time she thought about unleashing that information vanished into the silence.

"And how is she doing?" Tom asked.

Michelle lifted her gaze to meet the expectant faces of the group members, finding a reflection of her own courage in their supportive expressions. Their encouragement fueled her determination to share her story, knowing she'd be accepted.

"Honestly, sometimes I feel like it's a lost cause," she admitted.

"Why would you say that?" asked the young Black woman sitting directly across from her. Her tone wasn't offended or horrified, but compassionate.

"Like I told you all," Michelle started, her voice heavy, "Ellen is thirty-nine and still lives with me. She can't keep a job, and her drinking is out of control. She even sneaks alcohol when I'm out tutoring a student." She sighed, feeling strangely relieved after sharing her worries out loud. "She rarely ventures out, has no friends, and spends her days either asleep or glued to the TV."

"Is she seeing a psychiatrist?" Perry, the man seated beside her, chimed in. Despite his unlined face and unshadowed eyes, his prematurely balding head gave him an aged appearance.

"Yes, but I'm not sure the psychiatrist is doing much good. She's definitely less *angry* than she was before she started her new medication, but there are some things that...I don't know... seem even worse than before."

"For instance?" Tom asked.

Michelle almost whispered, "She's learned sign language."

"Did you say 'sign language'?" Tom repeated in a louder tone that prompted her to speak up. Several group members were actually grandparents, becoming a little hard of hearing as they aged, and wouldn't pick up on her murmuring. But she wasn't sure how much she really wanted to be heard.

"Yes. Sign language. When I asked her why, she explained that it's her way of avoiding conversations with people when she's out, like on a bus or in a store. She simply signs the words '*I'm deaf*' and believes it lets her off the hook. According to her, no one wants to take the time to talk to a deaf person."

"I have to be honest, that's a new one for me." Tom's gaze shifted around the group. "Anyone have any ideas, thoughts, or comments?"

"I do." The Black woman across from her spoke up again. "By the way, I'm Therese. Did she only learn to sign the words '*I'm deaf*' or did she learn more of the vocabulary for ASL? I have a cousin who's deaf."

Michelle chuckled lightly. "Just about anything she'd say in English, she can also sign. In case she ever uses it as an avoidance technique but encounters someone who actually understands the language, she doesn't want to be caught in a lie. So she learned as many signs as she could."

Therese tapped her palms on the arms of her chair and smiled. "That *is* pretty smart when you think about it."

"I agree," Perry said. "Do you have any idea how many times I don't want to deal with people? The sign language excuse is a brilliant solution. And the fact that she made sure she wouldn't get caught by someone who understands sign language? That's so smart."

Tom cleared his throat. "That is quite inventive. But honestly, is it the best way to deal with insecurity or even social phobia? She might avoid talking with strangers, but my psychology research and training has shown that interacting with people is an important part of one's healing process. If her daughter doesn't leave her comfort zone, she won't be able to live a normal life, whatever 'normal' might be. In this case, I'm concerned she'll never be able to live on her own."

Michelle nodded. "That's it. And it's why I've insisted that she visit her sister, Carrie, this weekend in Connecticut. She'll be traveling alone by train and staying with Carrie and her family for the weekend. It will force her to engage with people and potentially meet new ones. It's a way for her to step out of her comfort zone and experience some of the world. I really think it will do her some good."

Therese again tapped the arms of her chair. "If it's such a good thing, why do you look so...I don't know...burdened?"

Therese's insight surprised Michelle. A sudden surge of regret hit her. She'd been in this group for months and never spoke more than a few words to anyone. Why did she always feel the support inside this group was for everyone but her? Another question with no answer. But it didn't matter. Now that the focus was on her, and there was none of the judgment or mockery she'd feared, she was going to take full advantage of the situation.

"I pretty much brought the girls up myself. Even when I had a so-called 'husband.' Anyway, when it came to Carrie and Ellen, it felt like I was always making a choice. Carrie was always the popular one, outgoing, with lots of friends. Ellen was more introverted and kept to herself. For example, when Thanksgiving came around, since we had no other family, Carrie would want to spend it with our friends up the block or her friends from school. Ellen wanted just the three of us. I'd have to decide which one I should make happy. When we'd go to see a movie, Carrie would want to see an adventurous or funny film. Ellen wanted a drama or something sad. Again, I had to choose."

"We all go through that," Perry said. "It's part of raising kids."

Michelle laughed softly. "I know. And when I think back, those were the *simple* choices. When they got older, the choices got more serious. At seventeen, Carrie would go out with friends and do what kids do, including some drinking. When Ellen turned seventeen, she kept asking why *she* couldn't drink like Carrie did. Of course she could have. The difference was that Carrie drank while at a party or out with friends. Ellen never left the house and wanted to drink at home with me or by herself. That was another choice I had to deal with...do I let her drink alone at home since it was okay for Carrie to drink with her friends? Since I really didn't know how to handle it, I let her have a little now and then. She was already in therapy by then because she had only one friend, didn't want to go to school, and wouldn't join any social groups. It seemed like she was scared to leave the house. Then she complained that Carrie also cried and didn't act normal all the time. Which led her to question why *she* had to go to therapy and Carrie didn't. But Carrie had the typical teenager problems — moodiness, boyfriend issues, things like that. There was always something different about Ellen. Something darker. Something that needed more attention. So sending her to therapy and not Carrie was just *another* choice I had to make."

"Was there a reason Carrie might have *needed* therapy?" Therese asked, again without judgment.

Michelle thought back to the way her husband treated Carrie. She knew he'd made advances, flirted with her in his own sick way and frequently looked at her inappropriately. But he'd never done anything more. He couldn't have. Carrie would have said something. Ellen would have definitely said something. And she wouldn't have missed it. Absolutely not. No. Impossible.

"No, she didn't need therapy. If she did, I would have known it. She always had a good disposition, was very resilient and knew how to make the best out of a bad situation. She's either a very logical, stable, and happy person or she's the best actress in the world."

Michelle glanced at the surrounding faces in the circle, realizing she had been rambling on like so many parents before her. Despite the sense of relief after unburdening herself, it was time to bring her story to a close.

"So...in the end, Carrie has a beautiful family in Darien, Connecticut, and Ellen is living in isolation at home with her mother. Carrie would rather not spend time with Ellen because she says Ellen brings a bad vibe into her home. But she wants to give me a break, a few days of freedom. Ellen, on the other hand, didn't want to go. But I feel it's important for her to see her sister and nephew. They're the only people who will be there for her if something happens to me. And there it is, my latest choice: Make Carrie happy by allowing her to help me or let Ellen stay home in her comfort zone. Obviously, I chose the former." Her gaze remained fixed on her lap as she sighed heavily. "I suppose I'm just exhausted from making choices."

As she poured coffee into the white Styrofoam cup, Michelle felt the warmth of a hand on her shoulder. She turned to find Hannah, a single mother who had previously shared her own challenges navigating her daughter's borderline personality disorder. With a smile exchanged between them, Michelle finished pouring her coffee, adding cream and two teaspoons of sugar.

"You've got a sweet tooth, huh?" Hannah said.

Michelle closed her eyes, savoring the flavor and warmth as she took a sip. "Mmmm, guilty as charged. And it gives me that extra jolt of energy."

Hannah dropped a tea bag into her own Styrofoam cup. The aroma wafting into the air, pleasantly herbal. She leaned back against the table, both of them observing the cluster of parents engaged in conversation at the room's center.

"You know, I had my own dilemma with choices," Hannah said, a trace of sadness in her voice. "It's a tug-of-war. When you make one happy, the other feels left out."

"Yes — yes, exactly." Michelle took another sip of coffee. Finally, someone else understood what she'd been going through, the tangled web of emotions she'd been caught in for so long. She silently berated herself for not opening up about her troubles sooner. "So, what do you do?" she asked. "How do you cope with it all?"

Hannah shifted her gaze toward the table, her index finger tracing patterns on the paper cloth covering it. Michelle caught sight of a single tear rolling down Hannah's cheek. She tried to comfort Hannah by placing her hand on her shoulder just as Hannah had touched her before.

"I don't do anything anymore," Hannah confessed. The shoulder under Michelle's hand slumped, carrying a weight of resignation. "There's nothing left to handle."

Her heart clenched, her hold on Hannah tightening in a mixture of compassion and anguish. "What do you mean?"

Hannah wiped away the tear and locked eyes with Michelle. "Jeremy took his own life two years ago," she said. "There are no more choices to make."

Michelle placed her coffee cup on the table and wrapped her arms around Hannah. As Hannah returned her embrace, breathing heavily into her ear, her own eyes burned and went wet and blurry. Closing them, she allowed the tears to flow — uncertain if she was crying because of this near-stranger's tragedy, or her own guilt-ridden relief at the thought of what it would mean to be free of choices if Ellen pursued the same fate as Jeremy.

CHAPTER FOUR

Carrie trembled, cold seeping into the car and chilling her to the bone.

Gray clouds loomed over the train station and spilled snow as barren trees swayed in the frigid breeze. In their shivering, they almost seemed as anxious as she was. She turned up the heater, and with a soft hum it offered a temporary respite from the wintry March weather.

In the rearview mirror, she caught sight of Jack unfastening the top snaps of his coat with one hand. All the while he remained engrossed in his phone, his thumb tapping away like hooves on a racetrack.

"Feeling too hot?" she asked.

He shook his head. "Nah."

She peered through the windshield, spotted with tiny puddles from melted snowflakes. After she clicked on the wipers for a single cycle, the activity outside became clearer. Bundled-up people hurried from the trains, through the biting cold and into the shelter of the station.

She never really felt comfortable in Ellen's presence. Was it her ornery attitude? The secrecy she wrapped around her life — or lack of one? Was it the trouble that seemed to follow her wherever she went?

Like the stray dogs she'd feed and let roam the house, leaving her mother to clean up their messes and bring them to a shelter. The fights she'd get into at school — many of them leading to detention, one actually ending with Ellen's expulsion for a full week. Or the DUI she had less than a year ago that suspended her license for thirty days.

She couldn't find the exact answer to her trepidation when it came to Ellen, but as she waited for the train, she braced herself for the unpredictable and challenging moments that lay ahead.

Over the drone of the car's engine and Jack's incessant texting, a sound caught Carrie's attention — a whistle and the clack of wheels on the rails. She turned to Jack.

"Honey, the train is coming. Please put the phone away and pay attention to your aunt. She's here to visit you, too, you know."

He glanced up briefly. "And?"

"And she's family. So be nice to her."

"But what if —"

"No 'ifs' about it. You're an incredible actor. So it doesn't really matter if you like Aunt Ellen or not. Just act like you do and put on your best show. It's only for two days. I think you can handle it."

She turned back to the windshield but felt him observing her reflection in the mirror. When she glanced in it, she saw him rubbing his chin as if in deep thought.

"Hmm...playing the role of a nephew who likes his crazy aunt," he pronounced bombastically. "That's quite a part. But I think I can do it. I mean, I did play Pinocchio, for God's sake."

Carrie reached over the back seat, pretending to slap his legs. "You're terrible! Just be nice."

As the train gradually slowed down and entered the station, Carrie's heart raced, the humor she'd shared with Jack replaced by uncertainty.

She swung open the car door and stepped out, her eyes fixed on the platform. And there she was, Ellen, stepping off the train with her distinctive wave, her hand flailing up and down rather than side-to-side. Frantically, Carrie waved back, taking the chance to release some pent-up nervous energy.

"Ellen!" she yelled. "Over here!"

As Ellen turned in Carrie's direction, still waving, her stuffed travel bag slipped off her arm. The wind spat snowflakes in Carrie's face, and she ducked back into the car.

"What's wrong with her?" Jack asked. "She looks like a skeleton with sunglasses."

"Jack! We discussed this. Nothing is wrong with her. She's just a little thin and hasn't been feeling well."

Carrie closed her eyes, conjuring up more explanations. Jack had a point — Ellen appeared even more frail and unhealthy than the last time she'd seen her. As soon as she had some alone time, she'd call their mother and talk about it. Maybe, spending so much time with Ellen, Michelle hadn't noticed the drastic change in her daughter's appearance. Or... had she simply given up?

"I told you, it's like when you're sad or upset about something and you're not hungry and don't want to hang out with your friends. That's what Aunt Ellen is going through. So have a little sympathy. Put yourself in the role of a caring nephew. Like you said, you're a good enough actor to do it."

"Okay, okay! But now I know why Dad calls her ugly."

"Jack! I told you not to say those things —"

Her voice trailed off as she saw Ellen engaging in sign language with a stranger.

"What in the world?" she whispered, opening her door. She stepped out and walked toward her sister. As she approached, the woman Ellen had been talking to went on her way.

Though the day was dismal without a hint of sunshine, Ellen wore oversized sunglasses covering half her face. Carrie put her arms around her, and even through Ellen's thick goose down parka, she felt the bones of her back and shoulders. *Definitely need to talk to Mom about this.* She was unsure if Ellen held her to return the embrace or because she needed the support.

Once inside the car, Ellen removed her sunglasses and looked at Jack.

"Hey," she said, as if they had last seen each other just a few hours ago.

"Hey," Jack replied, his voice trembling slightly. His joking demeanor had disappeared and the inflection in his tone concerned Carrie. She wondered if it was Ellen's presence in particular that might be making him anxious or that there was now a semi-stranger in the car with them and he felt uncomfortable.

"I didn't know you used sign language," Carrie said, unable to contain her curiosity. "Who was that you were talking with?" She barely dared hope that her sister was learning to open up, maybe even making friends.

Ellen peered out the window, scanning the crowd — maybe for the other woman. "I have no idea, but let me tell you, she sat next to me on the train and I could tell within the first five seconds that she was a talker. So, I signed to her that I was deaf."

Carrie rested her hand on the gear shifter.

"But you're *not* deaf," she pointed out.

"That's the whole idea, sis. If she *thinks* I'm deaf, she won't chew my ear off for two hours."

Carrie shook her head in disbelief and disappointment. "So let me get this straight: you learned sign language so you could avoid talking to people?"

"*Now* you're catching on! I'm surprised Mom didn't tell you about that. She tells you everything else." Ellen threw her bag on the floor and fastened her seatbelt. "The fucked up part..." She looked at Jack and then to Carrie. "Ooops. Sorry. I meant, the *screwed up part* is that the woman actually knew sign language and I had to talk with my hands almost the entire trip. At one point, I wanted to use my hands to slap her rather than speak to her!"

"Wow!" Jack said. "That's cool! I want to learn too."

Carrie raised an eyebrow at him in the rearview mirror. "Aunt Ellen didn't come here to teach you sign language, Jack."

She wanted Ellen and Jack to get along, but teaching him how to be dishonest and giving him a potential tool to be antisocial was not what she had in mind. Her stomach churned. The weekend's challenges had begun and they hadn't even left the train station parking lot.

"It's alright," Ellen said. "I don't have to teach him everything. Just the important stuff."

"You mean like curse words?" Jack asked with a mischievous grin.

"Jack!"

"No, definitely not curse words." Ellen laughed.

As she turned around, Carrie caught the wink her sister directed at Jack.

Oh shit, here we go.

The restaurant was dimly lit, the authentic history behind its Italian decor established by photos of the owner's ancestors hanging on the walls. Wine racks presented an impressive selection of regional vintages and shelves behind the bar proudly showcased bottles of Italian liqueurs and spirits.

Carrie took a sip of her Cabernet as she eyed Andrew, seated across the circular table draped in a pristine white tablecloth. The flickering candle cast a soft glow across his handsome face, from his straight nose to his chiseled cheekbones and perfect lips. Yet even the cozy atmosphere couldn't mask or ease the irritation simmering behind his eyes. Carrie's gaze fell to the rust-colored floor tiles.

Their entrees were yet to be served, yet Ellen had already drained her second glass of Chianti. Her head swiveled with a jerkiness that reminded Carrie of a starving zombie seeking its next victim. She eyed every passing server, busboy, or bartender, anyone who could take her next drink order. When she spotted their waiter, Tomasso, across the room, she waved him down.

He raised his index finger to tell her he'd be with her in a moment, then continued taking the order at another table. Carrie's heart sank as Ellen rolled her eyes. Jack had been all too right about her emaciated figure. The hollows around the sockets were dark and deep, so that her eyes got lost in their shadows. Her sharply angled cheekbones seemed capable of piercing through her skin. Her thin lips highlighting her crooked, yellow teeth. What had become of the younger sister she played with as a child? The little girl who loved food, games, and telling jokes? Although she hadn't seen that Ellen in decades, Carrie searched the woman's face for a glimmer of her, a flicker of the person who had been missing for so long.

"May I get you something, signorina?" Tomasso asked, breaking Carrie from her reverie.

"Si, signor. Molto graz-grazi," Ellen slurred. "Can I please have a Grey Goose martini, straight up, no vermouth, please?"

"Of course, I will be right —"

"Oh...and three olives, pl-please. Just three."

Carrie turned to Jack, who stared at his aunt as he dipped his fried calamari into the bowl of red sauce in the center of the table. His face wore that same expression when he was trying to figure a chess move or how to stop the release of a catastrophic virus in his Spiderman video game.

"Of course," Tomasso repeated. "I will be right back."

Andrew dabbed his lips with the black cloth napkin he took from his lap, stealing a glance at Carrie before mustering a forced smile.

"I've never been able to mix," he said. Carrie should've been grateful he was attempting conversation, but the topic of alcohol, especially with the shape Ellen was in at the moment, was not a good one to broach.

"Not surprised," Ellen muttered, scanning the room again while she stuffed a piece of Tuscan bread into her mouth.

"Ellen!" Carrie hissed. She offered Andrew an apologetic look and took a breath. "Let's be nice, please."

Another eye roll from Ellen pushed Carrie to reach for her wineglass. She took a gulp and placed the glass back on the table, silently praying the entrees would arrive before Ellen's martini.

Unfortunately, there were two bartenders to help keep things moving, and as Tomasso approached their table, Carrie's hopes were dashed as Ellen's were fulfilled quickly enough to make her smile.

Tomasso set the martini glass beside Ellen's plate with a slight bow. "Your meals should be out in just a few moments," he said.

Carrie smiled in response and glanced at Ellen plucking an olive off the stainless steel pick with her front teeth. Her stomach roiled, and for a moment, she wondered if she'd be able to digest her chicken parmigiana.

"Actually," she said, knowing it was a bad idea, but unable to let it lie, "I'm surprised the doctor allowed you to drink... you know, considering the medication you're on."

Ellen chewed slowly, then swallowed the olive. "Like I would listen to the doctor if he told me not to drink? Like he knows anything." She took a large sip of her martini and placed it on the table, gripping the glass stem as though protecting it from being taken away. "Does Mom tell you everything? I mean, Jesus, if she tells y-y-you the medication I'm taking, what else does she tell you?"

Carrie didn't want to fight, especially in front of Jack, who looked up at her and cringed. She smiled and mouthed *"No worries,"* to him, then turned back to Ellen.

"Well, I didn't know about you learning sign language, did I?"

"You got me there," Ellen replied, taking another sip. "But she told my shrink. She actually called him to-to tell him I learned sign language so I wouldn't have to talk to people."

Carrie looked up at the ceiling, uncertain how to steer the conversation. Should she stick to discussing their mother or move into safer territory? Luckily, Tomasso and another server arrived before she could respond. They placed all their dishes on the table, and Andrew thanked them with a thumbs-up before they started to eat in silence. Carrie observed Ellen carefully, making sure she ate something. To her surprise, Ellen twirled spaghetti onto her fork and devoured the strands voraciously. *Thank God. Something to absorb all that alcohol.*

Chewing, Ellen turned to Jack and used her chin to point out a man sitting alone in a corner of the restaurant. "See that guy over there?" she asked around the pasta still in her mouth.

Jack nodded.

"What if he was deaf? Wouldn't it be nice if I could sign with him so he felt like he had someone to talk to?"

Jack nodded again.

"When you learn the language —"

Andrew interrupted. "But that's not why you learned the language, is it?"

Ellen grabbed the olive skewer and plucked off the second olive. Carrie could've sworn her teeth appeared yellower and more stained than they were an hour ago when they entered the restaurant. *Should've made her drink white wine,* she chastised herself.

"And how do you know that, Andrew?" Ellen asked, struggling to swallow her olive and speak at the same time.

Andrew set his fork down and took a sip of water. "Well, first, you just said your mother called your psychiatrist to tell him you learned sign language so you wouldn't have to talk to people. And second, you told Carrie at the station that you signed a woman today so you could avoid conversation with her." He eyed Ellen as if waiting for her to speak, maybe shock her into spitting out pieces of the olive she was having such trouble swallowing. When, instead, Ellen took another swig of her martini, he continued, "And your mother said —"

She swallowed hard. "My mother says a-a lot of things, Mr. Perfect. She even said things about you, like —"

"Ellen!" Carrie yelled. "Enough!" She dropped her knife and fork on her plate and surveyed the restaurant, embarrassed at the disapproving glares. This was precisely what she had feared, and she could kick herself for thinking this gathering could remain civil. Lowering her voice, she placed her hand on her sister's arm and gave it a gentle squeeze. "We want this to be a pleasant visit, Ellen. No fighting. No mean-spirited talk. Just a nice family get-together. Can we do that, please?"

Staring at her, Ellen slid the third olive off the skewer and chewed it with the precision of a surgeon.

"Absolutely," she said, punctuating the word with her martini glass slamming onto the table. "Abso-freakin-lutely. I'll make sure this is a nice...a delightful...visit from now on." She looked at Jack, cracked a smile and raised three fingers in a salute. "Scout's honor," she promised.

"What's that?" Jack asked.

She picked up her martini again and slurped down the rest of it. This time, she gently placed the empty glass on the table.

"I have no idea," she said. "But it's some sort of promise."

Before Jack could ask more questions, Tomasso appeared at Ellen's shoulder, his hands clasped, his gaze fixed on her glass. He stood between Ellen and Carrie, blocking their view of each other.

"Is everything okay over here? Do you need anything?"

Everyone except Ellen shook their head. "One more martini for dessert, please," she said.

Picking at his osso buco, Andrew shook his head. Carrie

considered canceling Ellen's drink order, but the way tonight was going, the attempt to reel her sister in would only end with her raising her voice in public for a second time. Instead she remained silent and focused on her plate. Suddenly, her chicken parmigiana seemed as unappetizing as Andrew found his veal shank.

Maybe if I have her move in, I'll shed those ten pounds I've been wanting to lose.

Carrie felt Ellen's gaze bear down on her, as if it could drill through her skull and her sister read her thoughts.

"Don't forget the olives, Tomas-so!" Ellen called with an extremely loud heartiness as if she were the only patron in the restaurant.

Carrie bit her lip. It was the only way to stop from spewing out her comments… and her chicken parmigiana.

If only she'd use sign language now, we wouldn't have to walk out of here with our heads down.

Ellen passed out in the car sometime on the way home. Andrew and Carrie lifted her out of the back seat and guided her through the door from the garage to the kitchen. They ascended all twenty steps of the main staircase, navigated down the left hallway and carefully placed her on the twin bed she'd chosen in the guest room. Once Ellen was settled, Andrew stormed out. Carrie gingerly removed Ellen's sneakers and covered her with a goose-down quilt she pulled from the closet. Ellen emitted a soft moan.

"Shhh…" Carrie hushed, tucking the quilt beneath her chin. "Shhh… go to sleep. We'll see you in the morning."

Ellen rolled onto her side, away from the bedside lamp, and drifted back into slumber.

Shaking her head, Carrie went to leave the room. As she approached the door she noticed Ellen's travel bag perched on the gray suede swivel chair. She listened for a moment to her sister's deep breathing, then picked it up, unlatched the straps, and held it up to the hallway light as she rummaged through its contents. Two rolled-up shirts, one neatly folded pair of jeans, toothpaste, a toothbrush, and a pair of ankle socks greeted her. *That's it?* Carrie unsnapped an inside pocket, searching for something she might have missed — Ellen may have stashed eyeliner, lipstick, mascara, any makeup. However, there was nothing in the hidden compartment aside from a light brown leather journal with a long, golden suede cord and attached pen. Briefly, Carrie thought about reading it. Did Ellen write about herself? About Carrie? About their mother? She teetered on the brink of unwrapping the cord, but then hesitated.

Would I want someone reading my *most personal thoughts?*

The answer resounded inside her head and without a moment's further thinking, she returned the journal to its pouch and snapped the bag shut. *Enough snooping.* She switched off the guest room light and closed the door behind her.

Walking down the hallway, she passed by Jack's room where he sat at his desk staring at the laptop screen before him.

"Hey," she said.

"Hey." He looked up at her.

"I'm sorry you had to see that. Aunt Ellen's just a little..."

Jack turned back to his screen. "I know. I know. She's got problems."

Carrie couldn't find the strength to come up with any more excuses for her sister's behavior. She was exhausted. Her body ached for sleep, her mind for solace. She walked to Jack and kissed the top of his head.

"Goodnight, honey. I love you."

Jack continued staring at the screen.

"Love you, too."

When she entered her own bedroom, Andrew, wearing only his Calvin Klein briefs, leaned against the bathroom door frame. He seemed about to speak, but Carrie raised her hand and shook her head, stifling any words.

"One night down, one more to go," she said, sliding off her high heels and aiming them toward the closet.

Andrew turned and went into the bathroom. "That's one night too many."

CHAPTER FIVE

C arrie opened the oven to check on the broiling chicken. The skin was browning nicely and the aroma of fresh garlic and a squeeze of lemon filled the air. A surge of pride ran through her to be making a home-cooked meal for the first time in what seemed like months. Between the late hours at work due to the possible bank merger, attending parent-teacher conferences, picking Jack up from rehearsal and now Ellen's visit, she hadn't been able to plan a meal, let alone cook one, in weeks.

As she tightened the knot of the floral apron around her waist, she glanced at Ellen, who sat on a stool on the other side of the white quartz kitchen island. Carrie had wiped the surface down after breakfast so it was pristine, and it shimmered under the warm glow of the overhead lights. When she and Andrew updated it a few years ago, she'd designed her kitchen to have a luxurious yet cozy feel, only it was now being punctured by Ellen finishing her second glass of Pinot Noir.

Did she drink this much at home, or was she taking her "time away" as an opportunity to forget her troubles and drown herself in alcohol? Carrie hadn't yet been able to call her mother and ask about Ellen's daily habits, but her over-imbibing and lack of care when it came to her appearance would be at the top of her list to discuss.

She turned her attention to the bowl of cooling potatoes, already peeled and diced, waiting to be mashed. She grabbed the potato masher from the drawer behind her and pressed down with purpose, slowly transforming them into a fluffy mound. After adding a generous amount of butter to enhance the Yukon Golds' flavor, a splash of milk to make their creamy texture even smoother, and a pinch of salt and pepper, she took the whisk sitting next to the bowl and gently combined the mixture.

Ellen made her way to the freezer and grabbed the bottle of Ketel One vodka. She opened the windowed cabinet next to the refrigerator, took a rocks glass and placed it on the island before filling it with the colorless liquid.

Shit, Carrie thought, *she really* is *an alcoholic. Why didn't Mom tell me she drinks like —*

"Why am I here?" asked Ellen, licking the bead of alcohol that had dripped off the lip of the glass and onto her finger.

Carrie continued the slow whip of her potatoes. "Why are you where? On earth? My kitchen?"

Ellen took another swig and refilled her glass. "You know what I mean."

"Yeah, I know what you mean." She stopped stirring, letting the whisk sit in the bowl and slowly sink into the potatoes. "Well, you're my sister and we never get to spend any time together. Plus Mom said you haven't been getting out much, so I thought coming here would be a nice change of scenery. Was I right or wrong?"

Ellen shrugged and licked her razor-thin lips.

"I think Jack had fun playing video games with you today. Did *you* have fun?"

"Sure. I like that kid. He's got smarts."

Carrie smiled. *Finally, something nice to say.*

"Yes, he does. Takes after me."

Ellen ignored her joke and leaned her elbows on the island. "He told me he used to have night terrors. Why do you think he had them?"

The thought of Ellen learning about such a sensitive aspect of her family's life caused Carrie's muscles to tense up, her entire body stiffening.

Clearing her throat, she said, "Yes, he did. It's been three years since his last one, so things have been good."

"Ever hear of journaling?" Ellen asked, twirling her index finger along the rim of her glass.

"I have. I actually read up on it when Jack was going through...well, suffering with the...night issues." She remembered the book in the pocket of Ellen's travel bag. *Why? Are you the queen of journaling?*

"My shrink doesn't stop talking about how important it is. He says it lets you get all your feelings and thoughts out so they don't stay bottled up inside. Once they're out, you're supposed to feel better. 'Lighter,' he says. Sometime, he says, you can take what you've written and get rid of it. Tear it up. Put it in the shredder, if you have one. It's sort of like ripping up your problems so they can't come back to hurt you. Or you can keep them. Depends on what works best for you."

Carrie leaned back against the cabinets lining the wall

behind her. With her arms crossed, she stared at Ellen until she stopped caressing the edge of her glass.

"Do you journal?" Carrie asked.

"Not yet," Ellen answered. "I'm getting up the nerve. I told Jack about it, though."

Jack's problems were none of Ellen's business. "Why would you do that?" she asked.

Ellen took a sip of vodka. "Whoa, don't get so upset. It's obvious Jack is a very thoughtful kid, very creative, too. He seems to have a lot going on in his head and from everything my shrink says, I think it could help him."

"I don't get it." Carrie leaned forward, her palms pressing flat into the island. "*Jack* should do journaling, but *you* shouldn't. How does that work, Ellen?" She thought about stopping there, but couldn't help herself. "And I'd rather you not give psychological advice to my child."

"Hey. Carrie. Slow down." Ellen slid back on her stool. "First of all, it's not psychological advice. It's just something I thought he would like to do. And second, I'm fucked up. Jack isn't. He has a lot better head on his shoulders than I do. I wouldn't know where to start with this journaling stuff. Jack *would*. So give me a break. I'm just trying to help. I'm not sure why you're getting so bent out of shape."

Carrie wasn't sure either. Residual anger from Ellen's behavior last night? Her incessant drinking now heading toward the same outcome? Or was it something else? A chill ran up her spine provoking an involuntary shiver.

"Well, we don't need help, thank you." Carrie grabbed the bowl of potatoes and scooped them into an oval-shaped porcelain baking dish. Once it was full, she placed it in the convection oven above the one cooking the chicken. Her mind raced. How dare this woman offer *any* advice to Jack about how to handle stress? *Look at her. She can't keep her hands off the booze. She has no job, no friends, no life, nothing. And here she is telling my son he should journal! I cannot believe she has the audacity to —*

"Okay," Ellen said. "I'm sorry and I apologize. I'll keep my mouth shut about stuff like that." She mimed the closing of a zipper across her lips.

Carrie took a deep breath and attempted to salvage the evening. She tried emptying her mind of negative thoughts and all the rude words she wanted to hurl at her sister. That would only make things worse. She forced a smile and took a step back. Nothing to do but make the best of this situation she had convinced herself would work out. How could she have been so naïve?

"Okay, fine." She wiped her palms on her apron. "Where were we?"

"Not sure you want to go there," Ellen quipped.

"Oh, that's right. You asked me why you were here." Carrie wiped her clammy hands on her apron.

"Yeah. Are you dying or something?"

Carrie slapped the island so hard an apple rolled off the pile in the fruit basket. She placed it back carefully, her hands trembling with restrained anger. "That's a terrible thing to say! Why would you ask me something like that?"

"It's just weird. Ya know? We never really got along that well, especially since we were teenagers. And now you invite me over for the weekend. I'm just saying...people do that kind of thing when their time is coming. You know, they try to make up for things they've done. Make amends."

Carrie's stomach churned. *"You might regret extending the invitation,"* her mother had said when Carrie first brought up the idea of Ellen's visit. The words echoed inside her head like a badly cracked church bell that refused to cease its chiming.

"Oh, I'm sorry," she finally said. "I didn't know I had things to make amends for."

Ellen raised the glass to her lips, tilted her head back and drained its contents. With a swift movement, she grabbed the bottle and poured another round. Her stained teeth, crooked and unsightly, sent a wave of revulsion coursing through Carrie. A fantasy kindled of ejecting Ellen into the frigid night and pushing her down the driveway toward the train station. *Get out and never come back!*

"Would you like me to enlighten you?" Ellen's voice sliced through the air.

Vile sarcasm. Just one of the reasons Andrew despises you, Carrie thought. She took another deep breath and opened the oven door to check the chicken. Watching the light sizzle on the chicken's crispy skin, she replied, cautiously, "I'm not sure that's such a good idea. We'll likely just end up locked in a futile battle, each seeing things from our own perspective. In the end, it will only lead to anger, and that's not good for either of us."

"Whatever," Ellen said, the word dripping with bitterness. "You never wanted to talk to me about shit, anyway."

Carrie put her hands on her hips. "Why *are* you so angry? Do you *know*? Does it just come naturally or do you blame it on me or Mom or our sorry excuse for a father?" The tear falling down her cheek surprised her. "Jesus, Ellen. We grew up in the same house, the same circumstances, and yet it's like we come from two different families. Over the years, I've racked my brain trying to come up with something I might have done to hurt you so badly. What I could have said that made you so angry...at me...at everyone? For the life of me, I can only remember trying to help you...trying to be compassionate."

"Compassionate?" Ellen mocked. "What do you mean, 'compassionate'? Why would you have to be *compassionate*? Was I a loser or something?"

Be careful. She's trying to trap you.

Instead of succumbing to anger, Carrie responded in a soft voice. "Why are you doing this, Ellen? You know we all have our shit. Do you think growing up in that house was a picnic for me?"

Ellen took another swig of vodka. "More like a smorgasbord...a buffet, if you will. And now obviously picking and choosing what you want to remember and what you want to bury."

Carrie feigned laughter, a strained attempt to diffuse the tension. "If only you knew."

"Knew what, Carrie? That you had a boyfriend since you were twelve years old? That I had moustache hairs growing like weeds while you had friends growing on trees? Did I see how differently our mother looked at you compared to the way she looked at me? And still does? Or when I was like seven, did I overhear them talking about how they should have stopped having kids after you? Is that what I should know?"

"That's absolutely untrue." Carrie's voice rose. "They loved you. *Mom* loved you. She still does. You...you..."

"I what?" Ellen demanded.

Answering that question wouldn't do any good.

"I *what*, Carrie?"

She sighed, exhausted from this conversation and the entire day. "You just never knew how to love her back. How to love anyone back. I'm not blaming you. It's just the way you are. I know it's not your fault."

Ellen finished the remaining vodka in her glass, but sluggishly. She reached for the bottle, but Carrie intercepted, gently taking it from her hand.

"I think you've had enough," she said, placing the bottle at the edge of the kitchen island.

Ellen rose from her seat and took unsteady steps toward the vodka now in front of Carrie on the side of the island. She lifted the bottle, and just as she began pouring, abruptly stopped and locked her gaze into Carrie's eyes. "Yes, I've had enough."

She left the kitchen. Carrie followed her into the living room, where she found Ellen turning her head from side to side. "Jack," she shouted. "Where are you? Time to kick some ass on that *Blasters of the Universe* game!"

Carrie watched her sister disappear, her tears washing her face. They came, she could admit, from both relief and sorrow. She glanced up, grateful that Andrew hadn't returned from work yet. If he'd been in his office upstairs, he would have heard everything. She teetered on the edge of emotional stability, and his "I told you so" would be enough to push her over.

———

Later that night, Andrew knocked on Jack's open bedroom door. Without waiting for permission to enter, he walked in the room, sat in Jack's desk chair and swiveled back and forth with childlike enthusiasm.

Sitting up in bed reading his script, Jack rolled his eyes. "You're acting like a two-year-old, Dad, you know that, right?" he asked.

Andrew stopped his playful movements and met his son's eyes.

I love this kid. Attempting to hide his true feelings, he replied, "And *you're* speaking to your father with disrespect."

"If the disrespect fits," Carrie chimed in from the bedroom door.

Andrew and Jack exchanged amused smiles as she made her way to Jack's bed. Sitting down at the edge, she massaged his feet through the soft quilt. He smiled and giggled softly.

"It doesn't fit," Andrew said. "Respect your elders. Especially your father who, along with your mother, provides for you. *And,* of course, the man who bestowed upon you all of his creative abilities. Including that amazing voice of yours."

Jack let the script in his hands drop onto his lap. He looked at his parents, a mischievous glint in his eyes. "Hmmm. I'm not sure I've ever heard you sing. Not one note."

"And you don't want to," Carrie joked. "Trust me. I've heard it. I have to be honest, you get all your talent from my side of the family."

"Ha!" Andrew snuck a look out into the dimly lit hallway. "*Your* side of the family? You mean, like *her*?" He pointed toward the guest room.

"Don't!" Carrie grumbled. "My great Aunt Martha was on Broadway back in the day. She did some singing. Actually had some solos."

"How come I never heard about this before?" Jack asked.

"Because Aunt Martha ended up in a loony bin, batty lip burbling," Andrew replied.

Carrie tilted her head. "What the heck...?"

"You know." He laughed. "When someone uses their finger

to make their lips flutter and then babbles? You know, like Hawkeye always does in *M*A*S*H* reruns when he —"

"Sorry, Dad." Jack lifted the script from his lap. "I'm not seeing it."

Andrew sighed. "It's sort of like blowing a raspberry, but you're using your finger to make a sound like 'brub brub brub,' like this —"

As he brought his index finger to his lips, Carrie put her hand up. "*Don't*, Andrew. It's not nice and it's not true." She looked at the braided wool rug on the side of Jack's bed. "Okay, well, maybe it is true, but no one ever really talked about it after she...after we never saw her again. All I know for certain is that she *was* on Broadway, and I'm still shocked that you actually came up with the term 'batty lip burbling'."

Andrew grinned. "You learn all sorts of amazing things working at an ad agency. Especially when you have to get TV commercial actors to do those kinds of gestures. I've got lots more." He twirled his seat. "Speaking of burbling and babbling, is she sleeping?"

Carrie looked up at Jack, who appeared to be awaiting the answer as well.

"That's not nice, and I left her in the guest bathroom brushing her teeth."

"Oh, she brushes those things?"

"Andrew!" Carrie shouted in a whisper. "Please!"

"Well, she could barely stand up from the table tonight. I mean, is there *any* liquor left in this house or did she completely clean us out?"

Jack didn't wait for Carrie to answer. "She talked to me about journaling. I looked it up and think it's a good idea. I'm going to start doing it on my laptop."

"What? You mean like, 'Dear Diary, Today I went to the store and —'" Andrew teased.

"No, Dad." Jack interrupted. He threw his script back onto his lap. "It's not like a 'Dear Diary' thing. It's where you write your feelings and thoughts down, just to get them out of your head and into words. From what I read online, it lets you understand them more clearly and helps with stress and anxiety. Lets you get better control of your emotions. I can definitely use that in my acting."

A pang of fear shot through Andrew's gut. He glanced at Carrie and then back at Jack. "Are you okay, son? Feeling overwhelmed by the play...anxious? If you need to talk to someone, we can always call Doctor —"

"I'm fine, Dad," Jack said. "I'm fine. It's just something that I think can help, like I said, with everyday stuff *and* with acting."

Carrie rubbed Jack's foot with more intensity. "Just because your Aunt Ellen said her therapist told her to do it doesn't mean *you* have to do it. You know that, right? I mean, Aunt Ellen doesn't even do it herself. She said she doesn't know how."

"She told me the same thing," Jack said, flicking the edges of his script pages. "But she said I'm smarter than she is and would know how to do it better. I'm going to set up a folder on my laptop and give it a try."

Carrie sighed. "From what I understand, isn't it better if you use a pen and paper rather than a keyboard? It allows you to use more of your senses...or something like that. Did you read that in any of your search results?"

Jack smiled. "Yeah, I did. But I can barely hold a pen anymore. I type so fast, I can get my thoughts out sooner. If I tried to write, I'd get too frustrated." He nodded like a judge delivering a verdict. "I'll see how it goes and then decide if I should go from typing to using a pen. The other thing is, some people like to get rid of everything they wrote once they're done. It's like you're throwing away your problems and bad feelings. And it's a lot easier to hit the delete button on my laptop than to cut or shred paper, right?"

"Sure. You know, I used to have a diary when I was a kid," Andrew said.

"It's not a diary!" Jack and Carrie said simultaneously.

They laughed together until a strange sound echoed from the hallway. They all fell silent, the only noise in the room the ticking of square retro clock hanging on the wall beside the window. After a few seconds, they heard the sound again.

"Carrie?" Ellen asked.

Andrew stood, recognizing a desperate and frightened tone in her voice. "Shit," he said. "I'll go see what —"

Before he could finish his sentence, he heard a distant thud, like the faint clap of a faraway thunderstorm. Andrew moved toward the door and pulled it a bit further open. There was another thud, still somewhat muted and impossible to identify. And another. And that was when it hit him, and his heart skipped a beat.

Twenty steps, one at a time, a series of irregular, rhythmic bumps sickeningly conveyed the motion and trajectory of Ellen's fall.

Carrie yelled her sister's name and, pushing Andrew aside, ran into the hallway. He went after her, and behind them he heard Jack jumping out of bed and following his parents. Along with the thumps, they heard Ellen's stuttering voice — incoherent cries, gasps, and strained screams. She reached the bottom with a final, resounding thud that gave way to a deafening silence.

Andrew switched on all the lights to full intensity to see Ellen lying flat on her back at the bottom of the steps. She held her upper right arm with her left hand and let out a guttural moan that reminded him of when he was a teenager and hit a raccoon with his car. He'd jumped out, as if he could help the poor animal, and heard its dying anguish.

Carrie ran down the steps as quickly as her legs would take her, but kept a hold on the banister. *Smart thinking,* Andrew thought. Even though Ellen had probably fallen because she was drunk, the last thing they needed was both women getting hurt.

"I think it's broken," he heard her groan. "It feels broken."

"Shhh..." Carrie crouched beside her and stroked Ellen's hair. "Lie still. We have to make sure everything else is okay before we try to stand you up."

Andrew watched as Jack ran down the steps, took Ellen's arm and rubbed it gently. He knew he should join them, but he couldn't get his feet to move. The anger and frustration swelling in his gut crushed his compassion. He searched inside himself, but couldn't find anything to help move his body toward the pathetic woman lying twenty steps below. *She* did this. *She's* the drunk. Why should I have to help her?

Damn it, Andrew grumbled to himself. Now they had to bring her to the hospital, deal with X-rays, MRIs, wait for results and who know what else? *Then* what? Would she have to stay at the hospital? Go home to her mother? Recuperate at their house? For a flash of a second he wondered if she'd done this on purpose.

"Andrew!" he heard Carrie call as his mind twisted in every direction. "Can I get some help here, please?"

He shook his head. "I didn't know we needed to put up the

baby gate." He took in a quick breath, astonished that the thought actually escaped his mouth.

He looked at Carrie whose eyes sliced into his. "Help us, please. Now!"

Still shaking his head, Andrew took one heavy step after another, somewhere inside hoping he'd never reach the bottom.

Tomorrow...she was supposed to be gone tomorrow.

CHAPTER SIX

A s Michelle walked down the stairs that led to the church basement, she strained to hear the group members. The acoustics played tricks on her ears, making it difficult to decipher who was speaking. But amid the chorus of muted sound, one voice stood out — Frank's. He was probably blabbering on about how amazing his son, Frank Junior, was doing ever since he joined the high school band.

Michelle couldn't help but credit Frank Junior's personality change more to his high dose of Lexapro than to the trumpets and bass drums. However, she kept her thoughts to herself. If Ellen somehow miraculously made friends or managed to hold down a job for longer than a month, she wouldn't want anyone quibbling about *her* victory.

If only...

As she made her way down the steps, her cell phone rang. Michelle leaned against the railing and rummaged through her purse in search of it. When she caught sight of the lit-up display, a tight knot formed in her stomach. The screen read *CARRIE*. It was too early for Carrie to have dropped Ellen off, which meant one of two things: Ellen would be arriving before she could make it to the station or something was wrong. Her intuition caused another twinge in her gut.

She tapped the green phone icon. "Hey, honey. How's everything?" she asked, then held her breath, not really wanting to know the answer.

"Hi, Mom."

Michelle heard fear in Carrie's tone along with a trail of exhaustion. "What happened?"

Carrie sighed. "Ellen fell down the stairs last night."

"What do you mean, fell down the stairs?"

"Just what I said. She fell down the stairs. Dislocated her shoulder and has a slight wrist fracture."

"How did it happen?" Michelle knew the answer before she even asked the question.

"Is there a reason you didn't tell me she drinks like a fish?" Frustration seeped through the phone's speakers. "She drank more alcohol over the past two days than I have in a year. What the hell, Mom?"

Michelle turned and trudged up the steps to the basement's entrance. When Carrie had first brought up inviting her sister for the weekend, Michelle considered telling her about Ellen's drinking problem. The words had been on the tip of her tongue then and countless times after, but the grip of fear they had on her kept them choked up inside. She was afraid that if she'd spoken up, Carrie would rescind the invitation, denying Michelle the break she so desperately needed. Now, guilt stung like a lash from the crown of her head and down her body.

"Why, Mom? Why didn't you tell me? I tell you *everything* and you don't tell me she's an alcoholic?"

"I'm sorry, Carrie. I thought maybe being out of the house would make her see things differently and she wouldn't drink so much." She gently bumped the side of her head with her palm as if telling herself the idea was stupid from the start. "I also thought that if you saw her drinking a lot, you'd be able to stop her because I can't. She doesn't listen to me. Just doesn't listen."

A cold wind spat in her face. She needed to get back inside, although she definitely didn't want the rest of the support group hearing this conversation. Michelle walked into the main area of the church and leaned against the frame of the doors into the nave. She looked up and took in the beauty of the stained glass windows, sunlight filtering through their intricate artwork in vibrant colors and sending tinted light dancing with shadows all across the walls, pillars, and floor. Despite the bad news in this phone call, the ethereal sight lifted her heart, even made her feel hopeful. Michelle hadn't attended church since childhood, but she wanted to stay there, lost in the splendor of her surroundings.

"You there, Mom?"

"Yes." Michelle shook her head, resisting the urge to slap herself so she'd snap back into the present moment. "So, I suppose that's how, or why, she fell down the stairs. Too much alcohol?"

"Exactly. To be honest, she's lucky to be alive. It's a good thing we know the best orthopedic surgeon in Stamford. His name is David Waite and he's a good friend. He moved his schedule around so he could perform arthroscopic surgery on Tuesday."

"But that's two days from now," Michelle said, more ruthless guilt slithering up her spine. "And does a dislocated shoulder really require surgery? Maybe I should come and get her. Bring her back here, and we'll go to —"

"Mom, no. David said there's a small tear on her labrum — that's the cartilage that surrounds her shoulder socket. He needs to repair it and tighten the tissues around the joint. It's not like he's slicing her shoulder open." Carrie paused, but it was obvious she wanted to say more, so Michelle kept quiet. "She's thirty-nine years old, Mom. You should treat her like she's thirty-nine or she'll stay a child forever. She doesn't need her mother running to her aid every time she hurts herself."

"It's not just that," Michelle murmured. "I don't want to inconvenience you any more than you already have been. Her visit was already a big deal, and now this? It's not fair to you. If I come and get her, it will make *me* feel better."

"Please, Mom. David has already adjusted his schedule. He'll perform the surgery on Tuesday, and then she'll recuperate here for a week, maybe less, depending on how she feels. Then you can either pick her up or she'll take the train home. She says she's okay with that. I'm just glad you have decent insurance for her and that she actually had her insurance card with her."

Michelle looked at the back wall of the church, where a gold-painted Jesus hung on an immense dark wooden cross. His expression of mingled pain and patient forgiveness almost made her cry, her guilt growing and then breaking in two — half went to Carrie for putting her in this position, and the other half to Ellen for not being there to take care of her.

Swallowing hard to hold back tears, she said, "I'm at my support group right now. Maybe I'll talk it through with them and see what they think." She heard both the attempt at apology in her own voice and, more surprisingly, hope.

"Good idea," Carrie said. "I'm going to make some calls to find someone to help take care of Ellen while we're at work."

"Where is she now?"

"In the living room, passed out from the pain meds. She's wearing a sling and wrist stabilizer."

"I'll try calling her later. Tell her I love her and I'm here if she needs me."

Silence hung in the air before Carrie said, "Okay, gotta run. Love you."

"Love you t —" Her daughter's phone clicked. "Too," Michelle whispered, the word falling into empty air.

———

After her fourth call to local companies offering caregiver services, Carrie's speech became rote.

"She'll be home on Wednesday and will need someone to check the dressing, make sure the incision looks okay, that she's wearing her sling correctly, and refill or help change meds if necessary. They should also monitor her wrist and ensure the bandage is tight enough. It's a three- to four-hour-per-day job for maybe four or five days. I'd rather not have her here by herself too long, in case she needs something. And yes, I know I'll have to pay for a minimum of a week."

Finally, Natalie, the owner of Natalie's Nurses, uttered the words Carrie had been longing to hear: "One of our aides just had a cancellation. He'd be perfect to assist with your sister."

"And his name?"

"Pete."

"Perfect!" She nodded even though the woman on the other end of her call couldn't see her. "Pete."

"Actually, he is Perfect Pete. He's precise and punctual. A real perfectionist."

"That's a lot of P's." Carrie chuckled. "My sister can be a bit...well...difficult at times. Does Pete also have..."

"Patience?"

"Yes." The laughter left her voice as she reflected, "The most important P of all."

"Yes, he does. No need to worry about that."

It sounded almost too good to be true. Carrie could only hope it was true anyway, crossing her fingers that things would go smoothly. By the time she called Natalie she'd approached the end of her list. There were few other options, other than asking a friend to take care of her sister. But there was no doubt in her mind that scenario would lead to the loss of a friend. Perfect Pete would have to do.

Ellen wouldn't be happy about having someone take care of her, especially someone she didn't know. That much Carrie knew for sure. But she also knew that Ellen wasn't able to take care of herself, so she couldn't leave her alone in the house for long periods of time. Carrie planned to adjust her schedule so that she'd be leaving for work just as Pete arrived at the house. After his shift ended, Ellen would be alone for a few hours at most. Maybe that alone time would help ease her resistance to having someone look after her.

Just a few days, Carrie. She'll be here just a few more days. Maybe this will make amends for whatever you supposedly did to her.

She took a quick peek into the living room and saw Ellen on the sofa, propped up and covered in the quilted throw blanket she placed over her earlier. Lost in a dream, Ellen's eyes fluttered; a thin thread of drool stretched from her lip to her shoulder. Carrie wondered what was going on in her head. Were the images in her dreams vivid and colorful, or as bleak as Ellen's perception of the waking world? Although she felt sorry for her, remembering their argument from the previous night helped Carrie suppress her sympathy, replacing it with anger instead. There was power in anger. She needed to stay strong to navigate the next few days, and pity wouldn't help her do that. Sure, Ellen wasn't as mobile as she was two days ago, but it wasn't her behavior that caused arguments as much as her words. And she didn't need much mobility to open her mouth.

Carrie quietly made her way up the stairs, taking them two at a time. They weren't particularly difficult to climb when you were sober. Glancing back at the living room, she made sure Ellen was still asleep before entering the guest bedroom. She retrieved Ellen's travel bag from the closet, tossed it onto the bed and unzipped it to inspect the inside pockets. When she found the one she was searching for, she unsnapped it and extracted the pocket-sized journal.

As Carrie unwound the golden cord, the journal opened to reveal its center page.

It was blank, pristine, as pure and white as freshly fallen snow.

Carrie ran her fingers over the book, flipping through the pages one by one, searching for any signs of writing. But they were all empty, untouched. She then checked for any ripped-out pages. Not a slash, not a tear in sight. Carrie blinked, questioning her own eyes. Miss "Journaling Is a Must" had never written a word in this sacred journal?

Apparently not.

Sure, she said she didn't know how to do it, but it appeared as though she never even made an attempt.

"Mom?"

Carrie's heart skipped a beat. She turned to the door, where Jack leaned against the jamb, arms crossed and left foot tapping on the threshold.

"What's going on?" he asked. "What are you doing?"

Shit. Should she lie? Confess that she was going through his aunt's belongings while she slept soundly and unaware downstairs? He'd caught her in the act, for God's sake. A criminal without an alibi, a mother with "nosy" scribbled across her forehead.

"I'm checking to see if I can help," she stammered, unsure how to respond to the inevitable follow-up question.

"Help with what?" Jack asked.

Carrie let out a sigh and gestured for him to sit on the other guest bed, across from where she sat.

"Help her with helping herself," she said, closing the journal and crossing her legs. Her foot tapped, like her son's had, but against the air rather than the oak floorboards. "It's apparent Aunt Ellen has some personal issues. I was just trying to find something specific I might help her work through — something that her therapist and your grandmother can't seem to do."

"So you were looking through her journal?"

Carrie's heart dropped. She was guilty as charged and couldn't summon the energy to fabricate some lame excuse, or deal with the shame of doing so.

"I'm embarrassed to say 'yes,' but I was," she confessed, her gaze fixed on the floor, her foot continuing its rhythmic tapping.

"If I start writing in a journal, how can I be sure you won't read mine?"

"I would *never* invade your privacy like that, Jack." The thought of his mistrust was a knife to the stomach. "*Never!*"

She felt her face flush and couldn't control her fingers from fidgeting. The boy was anxious enough without worrying about his mother reading his most personal thoughts. If she could only turn back time, she'd —

"Then why would you invade Aunt Ellen's?"

Carrie placed her hand on the bed to ground herself as her heart hammered. *Be honest.*

"I'll be completely honest with you, Jack. As you've seen, Aunt Ellen has some personal issues. My biggest concern right now is that those issues are causing problems in our home, within our family. Your father and I are arguing, which isn't good. And I'm not sure how her behavior is affecting you. There's unwanted tension in the air and I don't think it's good for any of us. What do I always say about the three of us?"

Jack pursed his lips and spoke as though reading lines from a script. "The three of us are like the three legs of a tripod that support each other. We stick together, no matter what."

"Exactly! And I won't let anything or anyone damage that support."

Carrie held out her fist, urging Jack to bump it with his own. "Our family comes first, right?" she asked.

Jack stared at her fist as though thinking through his options. Should he? Shouldn't he? Was he taunting her on purpose or playing a game? Carrie tightened her fists until her knuckles turned white. He finally made his way over and bumped her fist. "Right," he said. "The three of us come first."

As he turned to leave the room, he glanced back at Carrie and offered a smile. "I'm still glad I keep my journal on my password-protected laptop."

She rolled her eyes and glanced around for something to throw at him. There was nothing but Ellen's journal and she couldn't risk damaging it, so she shooed him away with her hand. "Get out of here, you little…"

He darted down the hallway toward his bedroom. "Password protected!" he shouted.

Laughing, Carrie stood up, her laughter dying in her throat as she caught her reflection in the mirror over the dresser. Her complexion appeared pale, her eyes weary, and her expression drawn with the anxiety knotting up inside her. *"Password Protected!"* Jack's words echoed in her mind.

"That's probably for the best," she whispered to herself.

CHAPTER SEVEN

E llen and Andrew sat on opposite ends of the sofa, tension hanging in the silence like a rain cloud about to burst, as they waited for Carrie to return with the pizza they'd ordered. He had already stoked the fireplace embers three times in the last five minutes; stirring them again would only make his uneasiness more apparent and increase the pressure in the room.

Odd circumstances had brought them together and Andrew couldn't — no, wouldn't — make things worse for Carrie. She was more affected by the situation than he was, and unleashing his anger at the drunken, foolish, immature woman eight feet away would only cause more problems for himself and his family.

Every now and then they'd glance at each other, only to quickly look away. Ellen would occasionally lift the corners of her mouth in a feeble attempt to mimic a smile. Andrew bit his bottom lip to keep his words inside. The slight pain helped distract him from the knot tightening in his stomach.

"I'm as happy to be here as you are to have me," she said, the sound of her voice jolting him.

Be careful. "I don't have any problem with you being here, Ellen. You should only travel when you're up to it."

"I'm just saying. I thought I'd be home by now and then..." she looked sideways at her arm and wrist. "And then this." She closed her eyes. "Trust me, I'll be leaving as soon as I can."

Leaning back into the sofa cushion, Andrew held his tongue. The same way he'd held it for the past seventeen years since the day he'd met Ellen, for what he thought would be the first time.

Two days after he'd proposed to Carrie, Michelle had invited them over for a celebratory dinner. He'd already met her a couple of times when she was also visiting Carrie's apartment, but her younger daughter was still a mystery to him. Carrie described her as "a bit odd" and someone "it took a while to get comfortable with." Whenever he asked her why, she'd shrugged her shoulders and changed the subject.

Now he sat in Michelle's living room, carefully squeezing a lime wedge into the neck of a Corona bottle. He took a gulp and before he could swallow, he heard footsteps descending the stairs. Looking up, he almost spat out his beer onto the coffee table. *Ellen Brooks? What the fu* —

"And there she is," Carrie announced, standing up. She approached her sister and gave her a hug. Over her shoulder, Ellen shot Andrew what could only be called a glare.

He stood but didn't feel strong enough to remain upright without leaning against the back of the sofa. As the sisters hugged, he tried frantically to devise an escape plan before they broke apart. But it was too late. Ellen was already advancing toward him.

"Andrew Hughes." She folded her arms and stared him down. "Long time, no see."

"Wait," Carrie interjected. "You two *know* each other?"

Ellen snickered. "We went to high school together. He was a year ahead of me."

Andrew closed his eyes, wishing that when he opened them again, she would have vanished, this entire ordeal turning out to be a figment of his imagination while he stood in a room with only Carrie and her mother. But when he opened them, she was still there, her gaze sharp enough to puncture skin.

"How...can you...I mean..." he stammered.

Carrie hurried over to him and clutched his arm. "Honey, what is it? You're white as a ghost."

He had to think quickly. "I guess I stood up too fast," he said. "I'll be okay in a second."

"Or will you?" Ellen asked, smirking.

"Ellen! What's that supposed to mean?" Michelle asked. She came toward Andrew and Carrie and hovered at his other side as if he might need her support, too.

Andrew took a deep breath and exhaled slowly. "There. I feel a little better." He shook his head and turned to Carrie. "I don't understand. Your last name is Pearson. How is your sister's last name Brooks?"

Her grip on his arm lightened. "Pearson is my mother's maiden name. After my father...well...after he was gone, Mom took back her old name and I changed mine to match hers. Ellen kept the name Brooks."

Andrew looked Ellen up and down, wondering why, in an instant, fate had turned so cruel. He didn't know what to say, worried that any words might provoke her.

"No more Chubsy Ubsy, right?" she asked.

The nickname triggered a flood of high school memories. The times he and his teammates mocked her in the hallways... threw food scraps at her in the cafeteria... stuck pig stickers on her locker. And then... Jesus... the time they tossed Chubsy Ubsy into the dumpster, and Ronnie Miller stood on the ledge and peed on her. Even he was repulsed by Ronnie's act, but did he stop him? No. God, why didn't he stop him?

He'd always wondered why no one else had stopped them. Why he and his group never wound up in the principal's office or thrown into detention. Why her mother or father never came to school to lodge a complaint or fight for justice. The only reason he could come up with was that the girl was too embarrassed to tell anyone, including her own mother, the humiliation she suffered every day.

Suddenly, Carrie's description of her sister as "a bit odd" made sense. After enduring such cruelty from him and his friends, how could anyone live a normal life?

"Chubsy Ubsy?" Michelle said. "Who called you Chubsy Ubsy?"

Carrie tightened her grip around his arm. "*You* didn't call her that, did you, Andrew?"

He looked at Ellen, wordlessly begging for her to keep quiet. She'd kept quiet for over six years; she could do it a little longer, right? At least until they had time to discuss it. He couldn't bear to lose Carrie over juvenile antics from so long ago.

"No, he didn't," Ellen answered for him.

The look on her face sent a shiver up the back of Andrew's neck. It held not only contempt, but satisfaction. She'd seen his plea and now they both knew he owed her. How she'd call in the debt, whether she'd make an effort to balance the scales, remained to be seen.

"I'm really glad to hear that," Carrie said. "But, Ellen, I've talked about seeing Andrew, why didn't you say you knew him? I mean, I told you his last name and that he went to our high school. Didn't you —"

"I moved here senior year," Andrew interrupted. "I barely knew anyone in *my* grade, let alone the juniors and sophomores. That's probably why she didn't recognize my name."

Carrie nodded, then released his arm and stepped between him and her sister. "Then how'd you know about that gross nickname?"

His heart pounded so hard it might burst through his ribcage at any second. Which would at least end this conversation. "I... I...didn't —"

"He didn't know," Ellen said. "I just said it in case he remembered me and what I used to look like. Obviously, though, I was as invisible to him as he was to me."

"You okay?" Michelle rubbed his other arm. "Do I need to hold you up a bit longer or can I go finish cooking the lasagna?"

He laughed and covered her hand with his. "Thank you. I'm fine. Go take care of the lasagna."

"I'll help, Mom." Carrie grabbed Michelle's hand and led her into the kitchen. Over her shoulder, she told Andrew and Ellen, "You two can catch up...or just see if you both know any of the same people. If I were just a few years younger, I'd be able to catch up with you!"

"Hag!" Ellen yelled to Carrie, her eyes still glued to Andrew. The tone of her voice was lighthearted, fitting the joke it was supposed to be, but since her glaring at him hadn't lightened up a fraction, it struck him as an insult. And maybe she intended that.

"Screw you!" her sister yelled back serenely.

Once the other women had left the room, Andrew opened his mouth, prepared to thank Ellen for not revealing their history to Carrie. She cut him off with a whispered, "No!"

She walked to the rolltop desk behind the sofa, grabbed a pen and paper, and scribbled something, writing as if the implement in her hand were a dagger. Finished, she tore the paper and handed the piece to Andrew.

He read a phone number.

"Call me at eight tonight," she said.

"But I wanted to —"

She raised her hand. "Nothing you want matters. I'm going in to help with the lasagna and drink some wine. Call me at eight... or else..."

As she left him standing alone in the center of the living room, her final two words rang in his head over and over again until it started to ache.

After three unanswered rings, Andrew felt a wave of relief. He was about to disconnect the call when he heard a click.

"Hello?"

Damn it. He stood up and paced his living room.

"It's Andrew," he mumbled.

"Look at you, right on time."

"Why did you want me to call you?"

"Wow. Right to the point. That's good. It'll save us time."

Her tone alone made his pulse quicken. *This is going to be bad.*

"You love Carrie?"

"Yes." He attempted to mirror the intensity of her tone, but failed.

"Well then, she can never know what you did to me back in

high school. If she did, she'd know what a rotten piece of shit you are. You'd be history in minutes."

"That's what I wanted to say today, Ellen. I wanted to apologize for everything —"

"Save it, asshole. The damage is done. You fucked me and now it's my turn to fuck you."

Andrew inhaled deeply. She'd been peaceful enough at the house and during dinner — mostly very quiet — and so he wasn't expecting such foul language. He'd hoped they'd be able to talk things through and make amends. Now he knew he'd misjudged. She was on a mission for revenge. He held his breath and felt like he was waiting for a punch.

"Carrie says you just got a good job," Ellen said.

"Yes," he acknowledged hesitantly.

"Here's what's going to happen. You're going to send me a thousand dollars a month for the next year to keep quiet. If you do, Carrie will never know what you did to me. If you don't, then my next call will be to my sister."

Andrew gasped and closed his eyes. "You're joking, right? Are you seriously trying to blackmail me?"

He heard a snorted chuckle on the other end. A sound that made his stomach churn. "Call it what you want, Andy. But Chubsy Ubsy wants her payback and she's going to get it from you."

Andrew collapsed onto the sofa, twisting a hand in his hair. Above his churning stomach, his heart raced. Was he having a panic attack? A heart attack? *This bitch is trying to kill me.*

"So what do you say, Andy? You love her enough or not?"

He closed his eyes again, looking into the dark behind his lids to try to find clarity and composure. Inhale. Exhale. Inhale. Exhale.

Just slow down.

"First of all, I can't afford a thousand dollars a month. I just started this job and am not making enough to give you that kind of money. Second, how can I trust that you'll never say anything?"

She cackled, the kind of sound he could imagine a demon in hell making as it devised creative ways to torture souls for eternity.

"I'll answer in the order received. I figured you wouldn't be able to afford it, but started bidding high just in case. Let's cut it in half to five hundred a month. That should cover what I need. Just think of it as another bill to pay. Second, as far as trust goes, you may think I'm nasty, evil, even the devil incarnate, but my word is my word. You hold up your end of the bargain and I'll hold up mine. It's only a year, then it's over. Totally up to you whether you want this marriage to happen or not."

"When do I have to tell you by?" he asked, stalling. Not that he could do much with that time. He couldn't seek advice on this without revealing what had happened, what an asshole he'd been. Guilt was already a heavy weight in his chest; he couldn't handle additional judgment. And what if he asked the wrong person and word got back to Carrie after all? This would be his cross to bear, alone.

"Two days. Then I spill everything."

Before he could even try mustering a response, he heard a click, followed by silence.

Andrew hung up and hurled the phone away from him. It struck the wall hard enough to leave a large hole and a crack extending all the way down to the floor molding. He crumpled in front of that crack and stared at it, arms around his knees. There on the floorboards, he rested his head on the desperate self-embrace of his limbs and started to sob.

Just another bill to pay.

And now, seventeen years later, he found himself beside the same woman who had urged him to trust her while she systematically drained his bank account each month for a year. Her words played again in the back of his head: "Trust me, I'll be leaving as soon as I can."

Yeah, sure, she'd kept her "Chubsy Ubsy" secret for close to two decades, but had she genuinely sought his trust?

The woman who used her mother's debit card to buy five hundred dollars' worth of lottery tickets? The woman who was supposed to pick her sister up at the Philly train station last year but forgot because she was too busy watching Star Trek *reruns? The woman who fell down a flight of stairs because alcohol is more important than dignity? Really... I'm supposed to trust* you?

He glanced at the clock on his phone. Rather than respond, he inadvertently let out a deep sigh as it was only 5:30, which meant Carrie wouldn't be home for at least another ten minutes. To ensure they made it to Jack's 7:00 dress rehearsal on time, they would have to eat and clean up quickly. And with Ellen grudgingly in tow, everything would likely take twice as long.

Andrew cleared his throat and broke the silence he'd created. "Are you sure you're up to going tonight? It must be uncomfortable for you. And your surgery is tomorrow. Wouldn't you rather rest?"

Please say "yes." Please...

With a smirk that spread across her face much more easily than her earlier attempts to smile, Ellen reached for the bottle of Vicodin on the side table. She shook it vigorously, causing an echoing rattle to reverberate through the room. "That's what these are for," she said. "They make it bearable, even if the surgeon said I can't drink because of the anesthesia tomorrow."

Andrew glanced at the sling on her arm, then at the tape and gauze encasing her wrist. All in all, the injuries weren't as bad as he'd feared when they found her at the foot of the stairs, but pain showed in her slouched posture, her body sinking into the corner of the sofa with her feet propped up on the coffee table. How did she even manage to get *this* far in life? No class. No respect. No social skills. *It's no wonder she spends her days at home drinking. I can't believe she and Carrie are sisters. What is wrong with* —

His phone on the arm of his sofa vibrated. It was a text from Scott.

"Oh, shit." Andrew sprang up and hurried toward the stairs, trying not to let his feelings show in his voice — his relief to be away from her, his excitement to see Scott's name on his phone. "It's work. I'll take it in my office."

The exhilaration was so acute that he didn't even notice if Ellen had responded. He reached the top of the stairs and settled behind his office desk within thirty seconds. With a smile, he tapped on the text, his heart racing with his brisk escape from the ugly tension downstairs and the thrill of receiving a text from his most passionate secret.

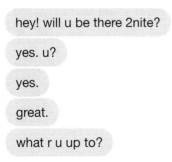

hey! will u be there 2nite?

yes. u?

yes.

great.

what r u up to?

> sitting with the nutjob waiting for C to get home. u?

> listening to Bonnie sing her Anita song. 'A Boy Like That.'

Andrew's smile grew. Oh, the things he could do with that line of text.

They would both delete the texts anyway, so he pushed a little, playing with a touch of fire.

> A Boy Like You. :)

> no. A Boy Like YOU.

> what I wouldn't give to —

Andrew stopped typing when he heard the front door open.

> C is home. gotta go. c u later.

> u bet.

> remember to delete.

> always.

Andrew selected the text thread and hit the trash can icon.

He waited for his heartbeat to settle before standing. He filled his lungs and exhaled slowly, hoping to release the last of his buzzing excitement, the deeper hum of his craving, and the intense guilt weighing him down.

Daily, Andrew rationalized his liaisons with Scott as not entirely his fault. He blamed nature; a faulty gene or a cellular mutation, perhaps. Yet no excuse shielded him from the shame that attacked his conscience. For a long time, he had tried to suppress his desires, burying them deep enough to remain hidden from the world and himself. Frustration led to bouts of anger and depression, unsettling mental states that frightened both him and Carrie.

All along he knew the reason, the burden he had buried so deep. But he couldn't share it with Carrie, and his silence left her confused and defeated.

But she wasn't the only one suffering during his battles with isolation. He'd spend those days and nights twisting his brain, searching for a reason, some sense behind his desires. After exhausting that route, he'd question himself, and then the universe. Was what he was doing right or wrong? Was it sinful or moral? Tragic or comical? As always, the answers were elusive and he'd gradually wrestle with his emotions until they were buried deep enough for him to reenter everyday life.

He enjoyed having sex with both women and men. It was something he'd carried with him since high school, if not before. He couldn't remember exactly. Despite his infrequent encounters with men providing a fleeting sense of completeness, he was always plagued by lingering regret and shame. But telling anyone would only inflict more pain on himself, judgment that would produce another gut-wrenching blow. So he established unwavering self-restraint, married Carrie, and promised himself and any God that might judge him that he'd abide by his oaths and deny himself these cravings. *Like resisting the temptation of that second cupcake or not purchasing season tickets to the Yankees games,* he thought, *I will not surrender to my desires.*

Even through the sporadic bouts of depression, his self-imposed arrangement had been working as planned — until he met Scott at a neighborhood block party two years earlier. It was a week after he, Carrie, and Jack moved into their new home. When their eyes met, Andrew felt that familiar twinge in his groin, along with something more, something that led to them holding the gaze before they reluctantly turned away to greet other party attendees. It wasn't just Scott's charm or physical attractiveness — his aqua eyes, chiseled features, or smoky gray hair — that pulled Andrew in. For those few heated seconds, it felt as though he was looking at a mirror image of himself, a man also shackled by the chains of what "should" be versus what "could" be. He recognized the same desire and frustration. Fate had brought two kindred spirits together and, in time, their families as well. With wives who both attended NYU, unknowingly at the same time, Carrie and Scott's wife Jamie had very similar interests. From tennis, chess, and clothes shopping to extensive participation in their kids' school PTA, the women became close friends almost immediately. Fate had again intervened, allowing Andrew and Scott to spend more time together — sometimes with, and more often without, their wives present.

It took nearly six months for Andrew and Scott to find themselves alone at Giovanni's restaurant, waiting for Carrie and Jamie to arrive. The women had spent the day shopping for clothes together, and Carrie called from Nordstrom's, saying they'd be late and asking Andrew to ensure Giovanni's held their reservation. When he entered the restaurant, Scott was already at the bar, sipping an almost full martini. Was it his first? Second? Andrew waved, attended to the reservation with the hostess, and then walked over. As he settled on the stool next to Scott, the bartender flipped back her ponytail with one hand and placed a napkin in front of Andrew with the other.

"I'll have what he's having," Andrew said.

Scott chuckled. "But you don't know what I'm having."

Andrew felt his face flush. He was relieved they were sitting in a low-lit area of the restaurant. The last thing he wanted Scott to see was his face turning red.

"I have a feeling that if you like it, I'll like it," he replied.

Those words seemed to be all Scott needed to hear. As he took another sip of his drink, he tapped Andrew's knee with his index finger and left it there. Andrew's heart raced like a jackhammer, pounding so hard he feared it might burst through his ribcage. He looked at Scott's finger and slowly raised his gaze to meet the man's eyes.

"You think?" Scott asked.

Andrew placed his hand over Scott's finger.

"I know," he replied.

They both heard familiar giggling from near the front door. In one swift motion, they pulled their hands apart. When the women reached the bar, a full martini sat in front of Andrew, while Scott held a nearly empty glass.

"Looks like someone took advantage of our tardiness." Jamie smiled as she kissed Scott on the mouth.

"Guilty as charged," he replied, stealing a glance at Andrew from the corner of his eye.

He hurried down the stairs to meet Carrie, who was setting the pizza on the kitchen island.

"You okay? You look a little...frazzled."

Andrew kissed her on the cheek. "Just ran down the stairs. A work call I had to take in my office."

Carrie nodded, taking the pizza box from the island and placing it on the wooden table in the breakfast nook. She glanced toward the living room. "How has she been?"

Andrew closed his eyes briefly, then forced a smile. "She's taking her pills. Lots of them. So she feels okay, I guess."

"No, what I really meant was how has she been to *you*? Nice? Nasty?" She leaned against the table, crossing her arms. "Have you two spoken or have you been keeping your distance?"

"She's been fine," Andrew half-lied. "I asked her if she was sure she wanted to put herself through going to the dress rehearsal."

A glimmer of hope crossed Carrie's face. "And?"

"She said she's fine with it. The Vicodin keeps her out of pain, so she's going to tough it out. Seems like she wants to go. Which seems a little odd...you know, seeing people, going out in public. Especially the night before surgery. Doesn't sound like her."

Carrie placed three napkins on the table and then opened the silverware drawer. "Sounds like the Vicodin, if you ask me."

Andrew took the forks from her and kissed her knuckles. "I should've set the table before you got home. You go sit with your wonderful sister while I finish setting the table. Then we need to get going so we won't be late."

About to enter the living room, Carrie stopped and said, "I'm going to make sure this is a pleasant night. That means I'm going to ignore *your* sarcasm and *Ellen's* misbehavior, something I'm sure will appear at some point this evening." She swept away the strands of hair falling over her eyes. "Are you sure you don't want to help her get into the kitchen? You're stronger than I am."

Andrew opened the windowed cabinet and took three glasses from the middle shelf. "Physically stronger. Not mentally," he quipped. "She's all yours."

When the cast of the play came out for their bows, for the first time in years, Ellen felt an overwhelming urge to applaud. But her useless arm hung in a sling.

"Damn it!" she exclaimed, slapping her knee with her other hand. Leaning over, she looked at Carrie, who sat on the other side of Andrew. Mascara ran down Carrie's face as she stood, clapping and cheering.

After the applause died down and the audience started heading toward the auditorium exit, Ellen glanced at Carrie and Andrew, who seemed to be waiting for her review.

"That kid is fucking amazing!" she blurted out, only to realize that her words were too loud to be swearing in a school auditorium. She shrugged and lowered her voice. "I mean, seriously. This kid is going places! Holy shit."

Carrie wiped her cheeks with a tissue. "Thank you, Ellen. He really is something, isn't he?"

"Takes after his dad," Andrew chimed in as they started making their way down the aisle.

Although she didn't want to dampen the moment, Ellen couldn't help herself. "You mean always acting?"

Andrew ignored her remark and squeezed his way in front of her, leading the sisters toward the backstage area.

Carrie gently placed her hand on Ellen's shoulder. "I'm glad you could be here tonight. I'm happy you got to see Jack perform. He loves singing and acting. Always has." She looked at Andrew who was about ten feet ahead of them, then back to Ellen. "Andrew's joke aside, I have no idea where he got it from."

Still walking, Ellen laughed and turned halfway around so Carrie could hear her. "Definitely not from our side of the family," she said, holding her thumb and forefinger less than an inch apart. "I came this close to crying when Tony died. I had to keep reminding myself it was Jack, and that I'd see him at home tonight." She faced forward again, her fingers still held almost together. "This close, I tell you."

The scene behind the stage was chaotic. Teenage actors still in costume, teachers, stage crew, parents — every corridor and side room was filled with people. In the midst of it all stood Jack, surrounded by at least thirty people, and Ellen started to panic. Just her luck if she'd be pushed around by the crowd and need surgery on *both* shoulders by the time the night was over.

Unexpectedly, she felt an arm embrace her good shoulder and turned to see Carrie beside her.

"I know. It's overwhelming with so many people and all the noise. We'll make it quick. Just a brief congratulations to Jack, and then we're out of here. It's even a lot for me."

Carrie's words eased the tension in Ellen's muscles, allowing her to at least pretend to enjoy the occasion. Finally reaching the center of the crowd, Carrie and Andrew both hugged Jack so tightly, Ellen thought she saw his face turning redder.

"Jack Hayes," Carrie said, "you deserve a Tony *and* an Oscar. You are absolutely the best."

Jack looked happy, but dazed, almost bewildered by the situation and the mob surrounding him. Ellen recognized that look, a sense of being outside oneself, overwhelmed by a mix of emotions. It was possible he didn't even realize it was his parents who were hugging him. With so many people around, so much noise, and an onslaught of compliments, for all *he* knew, it could've been the principal or janitor kissing him all over his face.

Ellen considered taking hold of Jack's hand when she saw Andrew peering across the throng of people. It was as though he was searching for something, someone. Who the hell could he be looking for that would... and then his eyes stopped moving, fixating on a particular spot. They softened and he smiled — a smile, Ellen thought, so bright and heated that it should have been directed at his wife, who stood only two feet away. A shiver of curiosity ran up her spine, and she raised herself onto her toes to catch a glimpse of who had put that expression on Andrew's face.

On the opposite side of the room stood one of the most handsome men Ellen had ever seen in person. His features were rugged, almost sculpted. His smoky gray hair was thick and styled like a model's in a cologne commercial. And his eyes. Even from across the room, she could see how strikingly blue they were, and they sparkled when they found Andrew's gaze.

Ellen slowly backed out of the crowd and leaned against the piano. Shaking her head, she rubbed her throbbing shoulder and concealed the smile that threatened to show on her face.

Holy shit. There's a lot going on here in Hayestown, USA.

Suddenly, she was glad to be staying.

CHAPTER EIGHT

S pending the night in the hospital had been a cherry on top of the shit sundae.

Lack of sleep, fake-smiling nurses, and a shoulder that felt like it was on fire pushed her dangerously close to the edge of losing her temper with anyone who irritated her in the slightest. Carrie, propping up the sofa pillow behind her for a better view of the TV, pushed her even closer to that edge.

"Jesus, Carrie," she told her sister, "I had nurses on my ass all night prodding me, pulling me, lifting me. They did a great job keeping me up all night. I don't need you doing the same thing."

She had pleaded with Dr. Waite and Carrie not to make her stay overnight, but the doctor insisted, wanting to ensure no complications arose. And as for Carrie, Ellen figured she just wanted her out of the house for the night.

Sure, they had gotten along well enough the night of the play, up until Ellen witnessed that look between Andrew and Mr. Cologne Model. Once she caught sight of their smiles, her mind had gone into overdrive, and she'd pulled back from the others, following them to the car wordlessly, as she tried to make sense of the situation. Was her brother-in-law cheating on her sister with a man? Did Carrie have any idea? Should she share her suspicions?

No, then Carrie would hate her even more.

Should she give her a hint?

You can't hint around that kind of shit. It is or it isn't.

Should she confront Andrew?

Nah. First, he'd deny it. Then he'd hate her more than he already does. He'd be angrier and act meaner but wouldn't be able to tell Carrie why because then his secret would be out. If it really *was* a secret.

She hadn't been close to her sister for years; for all she knew, Carrie had a thriving open marriage. Maybe she had lovers of her own. She'd always been adored by everyone around her, so why confine herself to just Andrew? And he, of course, seemed to have interests outside his marriage.

But Ellen didn't really think that was the case.

What about Jack? Should she tell him?

Nice kid, but he should know who and what his father is. Christ, who's the better actor in this family?

Her mind reeled, swinging between doubt and conviction.

She wouldn't say a thing... yet. Not to anyone. It would only lead to more family problems and people getting pissed off. And even though Andrew's infidelity was the core of the issue, *she* would get the sole blame. Just like she always did.

"Carrie." Ellen ran her fingers through her tangled hair. "You know that girl who played Anita Monday night?"

"Yes, Bonnie. She was great, wasn't she?"

Yeah, great.

"I saw her in the crowd around Jack after the play. Do you think he and she would make a good couple?"

Carrie took a pause organizing pill bottles and the TV remote on the side table. "What? Why would you think that?" She went to sit on the sofa.

"I don't know. They're both cute, young actors. Just thought there might be something up between them."

Carrie pinched the bridge of her nose and closed her eyes. "Jack doesn't talk to me about that stuff. Plus, he's fifteen. He's still pretty young."

Wait, weren't you giving Tommy Gates a blowjob under the bleachers at fifteen?

"I hear you," Ellen replied. It was time to get to the real reason behind her questioning. "Do you know her parents? I think I saw them standing with her after the show."

"Yeah, Jamie and Scott Madison. We're pretty good friends, actually. Jamie and I do a lot of things together."

Oh, this is getting good. Excitement fluttered in Ellen's stomach. Why? What did she gain from Carrie's misery? From potentially shattering the perfect Hayes family?

Stop thinking so much.

"What about Scott and Andrew?" she asked. "Do they hang out together, too?"

"Not as much." She stood, glanced out the window and exclaimed, "Pete's here!"

Ellen rolled her eyes. "I told you, I don't need an *aide*. It makes me feel like an invalid. I don't want someone here all the time."

"No one cares what you want," Carrie said, half in jest. "Dr. Waite wants you to have someone here. You're on some heavy meds, and he doesn't want you to undo his surgery by moving your arm in some way or putting your sling on wrong. He wants two full days of you not doing anything with that arm."

"But, I —"

"And with everything Pete will be doing, I'd consider him more of a nurse," Carrie explained, walking toward the door. "He'll make sure your incision is healing properly, that you're taking your meds, and that your sling and bandage are in place. It'll only be for the next few days until you're well enough to go home."

Ellen opened her mouth, about to continue the argument, but then the realization of Carrie's motive made her snap it shut.

Guilt, she thought. *She must feel guilty because of everything she did and didn't do while we were growing up. She's trying to make up for it now.*

Does she think a male nurse will erase all that shit?

"Hello, Peter," Carrie said, opening the door.

Ellen squinted, her eyes still pretty blurry from the painkillers and lack of sleep. From a distance, the young man appeared tall, well-built if a bit lanky. *Oh, like I have room to talk!*

"Hi there. Good morning to you both." He had a way of talking and a flourish as he removed his coat and put down his satchel that immediately suggested he was gay.

Hmmm...this could be interesting, Ellen thought.

As he neared the sofa, his features became much clearer. Dark skin and large, coffee-colored eyes revealed his Latino heritage. His nose was perfectly straight, the tip delicate, making his profile refined but not weak. When he smiled, his smooth, full lips opened to expose straight white teeth of the kind she'd only ever seen on television.

"Well, hello," Ellen said, scooting farther into the sofa to make room for him.

"Hello, again." He smiled and nodded toward Ellen. He turned and looked at Carrie. "Natalie told me you changed your work schedule. I've been updated on Ellen's condition and have everything I need from Dr. Waite's office. So if you have to go now, please don't worry. I have everything under control."

Carrie grabbed her coat from the armchair and slid her arms into the sleeves. "Oh my. You really *are* Perfect Pete, aren't you?"

Pete's gaze dropped to the rug beneath his feet and shook his head. "Far from perfect, but thank you."

"Thank *you*." Carrie opened the front door and stepped outside. Before she closed it, she turned and looked back at him. "You have my number if you need *anything*." Then her gaze and a pointing finger went to Ellen. "Behave yourself, please."

Once the door closed, Pete rose from his seat and approached the satchel he had placed on a chair.

"What did she mean, 'behave yourself'?" he asked as he unpacked his supplies.

Ellen snorted. "Don't pay attention to her. She's a Goody Two-Shoes. Now, how about you and I get to know each other? There's some vodka over there." She gestured to the liquor cabinet. "I just want a small glass. Even a shot will do."

Unfazed, Pete continued arranging his supplies on the coffee table. "Not on *my* watch, you won't."

"C'mon, Pete. You seem like a cool guy. Just a little —"

"Not going to happen," Pete said, taking a seat at the other end of the sofa. "*Now* I understand what your sister meant when she asked you to behave yourself. You're on an opioid, you had anesthesia yesterday. You need optimal blood circulation. Did you know that alcohol can constrict blood vessels?"

Damn, this guy is Carrie in scrubs.

Ellen pretended to be disappointed, adding a touch of tearfulness to her voice. "Wow, I thought you were cool."

"Cool or not, let's check your vitals."

She studied his face as he wrapped the blood pressure cuff around her good arm. Silky smooth skin, beautiful lips, and bullshit-free. *Of* course *he's gay.*

"So," she began, straightening her arm so Pete could slip the stethoscope drum between the cuff and crease of her elbow. "I love that diamond stud in your ear. It's small, but elegant."

"Thank you," he said, slipping the ear tips in.

"So, was it a gift, or did you —"

"Shhh." Pete hushed her gently. "I need you to be silent for at least a minute."

"I can handle that. I can be quiet for —"

"Clearly not." He smirked and pumped the bulb, his eyes glued to the gauge. After a few more pumps, he released the cuff. This time, a full smile appeared on his face. "Looks good. One twenty over seventy-five. I like that."

"Your teeth are so white," Ellen remarked, nearly smiling until her mind conjured images of her own crooked, yellowed teeth. "And they're straight too."

"Runs in the family." Pete's touch was delicate as he examined the bandage covering her incision.

"What runs in the family? Being straight?"

He let out a soft laugh. "You're something else, Ellen. And I know where you're going with this. So let's just get it out. My straight teeth run in the family. Obviously, I'm *not* straight." He carefully examined the dressing on her shoulder, lightly touching it with his fingertips.

She flinched anyway. "I just wanted to make sure."

"Did that hurt?" he asked.

"No, not really."

"Good." He gently lifted her to examine the back of the dressing. "Why did you want to make sure? Is there a problem with me being gay?"

She snickered. "Is there a problem with me being nutso?" She twirled her finger around her temple. "No, I actually had a few questions."

"Okay. But first, let's take your temperature, then check your respiration and measure your oxygen saturation."

Ellen's excitement made her smile. Though Carrie had hired this guy hoping to earn her forgiveness, her sister had no idea he'd be used as an important source of information. But she couldn't let on that's what she was after, so she feigned another flinch.

"Holy crap, I didn't have open heart surgery. The guy just cut me and worked on my shoulder. A little physical therapy, and I'll be good as new in a few weeks."

"Not my call," Pete replied. "I'm here for a few hours to ensure your well-being and provide any necessary help." He retrieved the Vicodin bottle from the side table, opened it, and counted the pills. After checking the label, he closed the bottle and placed it back on the table.

"You've been overmedicating," he said. "Are you in that much pain?"

Ellen liked this guy. She wasn't about to play games with him about the pills. It would only lead to an argument. Might as well tell it like it was.

"Yeah, pain isn't bad enough to overmedicate. I do it because it feels good."

Pete didn't scowl at her or roll his eyes as she half-feared he would. Instead, he crouched near the center cushion of the sofa, where her feet rested, and began to gently rub them. Between the pills and the free massage, she almost allowed herself a moan of delight.

"Do I need to lecture you about the growing problem of opioid addiction?" he asked.

"No, you don't," she replied, angry he'd pulled her from physical bliss. "Now, let's get back to you."

Pete raised his hand. "Just so you know, I'll be checking the bottle again tomorrow. It's my duty to report any potential issues. Got it?"

She nodded. "Got it. I'll get the dosage back on track. I promise. Now, can I ask you a personal question?"

"Depends. What is it?"

"If a guy acts straight, but isn't — like, maybe he's even dating or married to a woman — can you still tell if he's gay or bi?"

Pete smiled, continuing to massage her feet.

Holy shit, that feels soooo good.

"What's this about? Why are you asking me this?"

"Just curious," she said quickly, even as her stomach rumbled with anticipation. "I'm asking for a friend."

He sighed.

"Fooling around with married men isn't something I'd ever do, and I don't advise you to try it either. But if you mean how I can tell guys in general are interested, it's called gaydar."

"Gaydar?" Ellen repeated. "That's a real thing?"

"Let's just say it's intuition."

"Like a psychic?"

Pete laughed. "Not quite. I don't have ESP or read minds. It's more like when you walk into a party and there's someone you instantly dislike."

"I don't go to parties," she replied.

"Okay, so you're in a supermarket or bank or any place with people. I'm sure you've felt something like *ewww, bad vibe. Or,* you really *like* someone because your radar tells you they're just a good person."

"Yeah." She wanted to tell Pete that was how she felt about him, but she restrained herself. "Yeah, that's happened."

"Well, just as you can tell if someone is good or bad, I can usually tell if someone is gay or straight. Maybe because I'm gay. I don't know. It could also be —"

He broke off at the sound of a key turning in the front door. They both turned to see Andrew removing his sunglasses and patting his cheeks, which were red from the frigid air outside. He swiftly closed the door and rubbed his hands together.

"It's freezing out there," he commented.

"You know what they say," said Pete. "March comes in like a lion and out like a lamb."

"Who's they?" Andrew asked, walking toward Pete and extending his hand. "Andrew," he introduced himself. "Ellen's brother-in-law."

Pete stood and shook Andrew's hand. "Pete. Ellen's new friend and temporary caretaker."

Ellen observed Andrew's reactions like he was a specimen under a microscope. Did he have any peculiar response to a handsome man in his living room? Did he hold Pete's hand longer than he would a less attractive man or woman? Was he shuffling his feet because he was cold, or uncomfortable, or dangerously comfortable?

"Nice to meet you," Andrew said, his voice warm, but nothing more. He looked at Ellen. "And how are you?"

She pursed her lips and shrugged her good shoulder. He

didn't pay her any more attention than that, and she hadn't expected him to.

"Again, nice to meet you, Pete." Andrew walked to the staircase. "I forgot an important folder in my office. Came home to get it. Didn't have time to screw my head on this morning."

Ha! You didn't get to screw something *this morning,* Ellen joked to herself.

She watched Andrew run up the stairs and exchanged a quick glance with Pete as above them Andrew spoke on the phone as he closed his office door. Shortly after, he descended the stairs, buttoned his coat and stood to the side of the sofa.

"You rest up," he said to Ellen. "And nice to meet you, Pete."

Was that a wink?

"Bye," Pete replied, going to the door with Andrew. He locked it behind him.

Ellen tried to sit up straighter. "Did you say 'bye' to him or are you telling me he's 'bi'?"

Pete slid the wingback chair across the rug until it faced Ellen, sank into it and crossed his legs. "So is that the guy you were curious about?"

Ellen nodded eagerly.

Pete leaned back, rubbing his chin as if pondering the meaning of life.

"Cut it out!" she snapped. "Tell me what your gaydar is telling you!"

"This is a tough one," he said, grinning.

"Well, fine tune it, please."

"Okay, I'll estimate there's a ninety-eight percent chance he's bisexual."

Ellen's eyes grew wider. She leaned forward. "What about the other two percent?"

"Gay. But again, this is all speculation. He *could* be as straight as an arrow."

Ellen fell back on her pillows. "Or a French horn."

The clock on the side table displayed 4:00, and Ellen was engulfed in a sea of boredom.

Pete had left over an hour ago, and Carrie wouldn't be home for another two. Shit. If she were home, at least she'd be able to sneak a shot or two of vodka and listen to some music with a buzz. She'd even be able to go to the mall and invent nasty stories about everyone she saw.

Instead, she was trapped on the couch in this house, suffocating for lack of anything interesting to watch or think or do. Ellen took her phone off the side table, slid it in her pocket and twisted herself around so she could set her socked feet on the floor. Using her good arm, she held onto the sofa and then gripped the ends of its arm to help her stand straight. She was surprised at how good she felt: no dizziness, no nausea. The inability to use her arm and wrist appeared to be her only obstacles to getting back to a semi-normal life.

She peeked at the bottle of Vicodin. Pete's words reverberated in her head: *I'll be checking the bottle again tomorrow.* Fuck. She couldn't take another pill for at least six hours. If she took more, and he reported her, who knew what they'd do? They might lock her up in an addiction facility. How easy that would make life for both Carrie *and* her mother.

Her eyes went up the stairs and followed the catwalk to the door of Andrew's office.

Hmmm...a quick search is pretty harmless. I do *have to protect my sister,* she thought, not even believing it herself.

Holding onto the railing, she cautiously climbed the twenty steps. When she reached the top landing, she stopped to catch her breath, exhausted, but more relieved she didn't suffer the same fate as last Saturday night. She made her way to Andrew's office, poked her head in and then entered.

The room was bathed in warm, natural light that streamed in through two large windows adorned with Roman shades. The walls were painted beige, which must contribute to Andrew's ability to focus while he worked in here. The floor was covered with a deep-pile rug in muted earth tones, plush beneath her feet. Ellen figured Carrie must have decorated this room, since Andrew could barely dress himself without her. There was no way he could put something this nice together.

Across from the windows, a vintage-style bookcase housed a collection of books on marketing, advertising, and research. *Boring!* An array of trinkets also adorned the shelves: awards from work, achievement certificates and trophies from college baseball. *Time to grow up, Andy.*

A sturdy oak desk stood in the center of the room, its surface polished to a rich golden sheen. Its spacious surface provided ample room for a state-of-the-art Apple computer, high-resolution monitor and a sleek wireless keyboard and mouse. A small, elegant lamp stood at one corner, which probably helped him see his keyboard at night while he typed love notes to Scotty. A leather chair sat in the front of the desk and a more comfortable-looking one behind it, its worn appearance a testament to hours of working, writing, and probably daydreaming about his next tryst. Maybe it was one of those expensive ergonomic ones offering lumbar support. He must appreciate that when he sat in it for a private wanking session, thinking of Scott — or sexting him — and God knows who else.

Alongside framed motivational quotes and landscape paintings, the walls held photographs of Carrie and Jack. She had to hold herself back from gagging. The room felt like a lie, a place where Andrew pretended to work but really spent his private time with the door shut and his dick out.

A sudden buzz came from the top of his desk.

"Holy shit, he left his phone here." She spoke out loud in surprise at how stupid he truly was. *No wonder Carrie is the breadwinner. This guy can't remember shit.*

She walked to the phone and picked it up seconds before the ringing stopped. She tapped the display, but the lock screen required a password. Shit. How the hell was she going to get into the phone?

Well, the guy's a lame brain, so he's gotta have a lame code.

She entered Jack's birthday and got nowhere. Then she gave Carrie's birthday a try. Not accepted. Then Carrie *and* Jack's birthdays. No. Then the dates reversed. Still, the screen wouldn't budge. When she entered Jack's birthday, included the year and then their house number, 473, the black screen turned into a full-color display of apps and a background photo of Carrie and Jack.

"Bingo!"

Finding the text app immediately in the center of the screen, Ellen smiled at the notification bubble announcing four messages had been received.

"Who's this from?" she asked, tapping the icon.

When it opened, she fell against the desk. There was a selfie of Scott, wearing little more than a smile from ear to ear. That one only showed him above the waist, but Ellen swiped up to reveal another photo, this one of a smooth, round butt which she could only assume was Scott's. She made the same assumption when she swiped up again and saw a full-frontal view of a man's genitals with the message:

> When do you want more of this?
> Remember to delete!

She wasn't sure if the chill in her stomach was caused by excitement from the sexy photos or by the realization that Carrie's perfect life was a giant mess and she didn't even know it. Ellen slipped her own phone out of her pocket and took a photo of the text thread. *You never know,* she rationalized — to whom, she wasn't sure. As she tapped the ellipses to mark the texts as "unread," she heard a car pull into the driveway. She pressed the power button on the side of the phone, put it back in the same spot she found it and walked as quickly as she could to the guest bedroom.

The moment she plopped down on the bed beside her travel bag, she heard footsteps sprinting up the stairs and into Andrew's office. She was pretending to look through her bag when she heard a tap on the bedroom door.

"You came up here by yourself?" he asked.

"Yeah," she said, unable to look him in the eyes. "I'm fine. A little woozy, but fine."

"You really shouldn't go up or down the stairs after anesthesia."

She sighed, continuing the act of searching through her bag. "Weren't you just here or am I losing my mind, too?"

Andrew let out a forced laugh. "I forgot my phone. I swear, I don't know what's wrong with me."

Where do I start?

"Okay, back to work. See you later," he said.

He turned and hurried down the steps, without offering to help her down them, without asking if she needed anything before he left. He simply ran out and left her sitting on the bed, alone. Of course, that's what she wanted, but still...

What a no-good, rotten, cheating piece of —

The front door slammed below, cutting off her thoughts. Ellen pulled out her phone, opened the photo gallery, and laughed out loud as she re-read Scott's text. She zoomed in on his face, staring at the reflection of the camera's flash in his eyes.

"Oh, Scotty," she said. "You have no idea what you've just done."

CHAPTER NINE

Something wasn't right.

The four of them sat in the breakfast nook. Through the window at the end of the table, weak morning light cast a subdued glow on framed family photos. Ellen gazed outside at the snowflakes twisting as they fell, their frigid dance mirroring the icy atmosphere inside.

Today the strain between her and Andrew felt more palpable than ever. He hadn't looked at her once since they'd sat down. He never asked how she was feeling or even if she'd slept well. No matter the sounds she'd make clanking her silverware or slurping her orange juice, there was no acknowledgment. It was as though she was invisible, at least to him.

Did he suspect her plans? Could he read her thoughts? Damn it, if he did, she needed to come up with an alternate strategy.

"It's a little late in March for this kind of snow, isn't it?" Ellen remarked, spearing her fork into the stack of pancakes in the center of the table. "I thought they said 'March comes in like a lion and goes out like a lamb.' This definitely doesn't feel like a lamb to me."

Carrie got up as the coffeemaker finished brewing the last drop of a fresh pot. She set the pot on the trivet in the center of the table and settled beside Andrew on the cushioned bench. Next to Ellen, Jack spread butter along the top of his pancakes. As it melted, it dripped down the sides until it made puddles on his plate. Still he slathered on more. Ellen nudged his arm playfully.

"Need some pancakes with that butter?" she asked.

Jack chuckled and started cutting into the stack of cakes. "I just read somewhere that butter has a lot of calcium and other things that are good for your bones, skin, and even your eyesight."

Across the table, Carrie was washing down her pancakes with a slug of coffee as Andrew stirred a second teaspoon of sugar into his cup. They were acting just like they had every day since she'd been there, but something was off. There was a strange vibe in the air, elusive and so hard to pinpoint it made her head ache. *She* was the one with the ace so high up her sleeve that it was almost slicing her skin. *She* should be the one acting weird... or maybe she *was* the one acting weird and didn't know it.

The weirdness, she saw now, came from the space between Carrie and Andrew. Although they were sitting next to each other, they appeared miles apart. Not a word has passed between them since entering the kitchen. The coolness, Ellen suddenly realized, had nothing to do with her but everything to do with the couple sitting across from her.

They must be having a fight. But what about? Ellen hadn't noticed any issues during last night's dinner or when they sat in the living room watching TV afterward. Something must've happened after everyone went to bed... or maybe *nothing* happened and *that* was the root of the problem.

Carrie nibbled at her pancakes, then gently placed her fork on the rim of her plate, dabbing her lips with a napkin.

"Remember," she said, looking directly at Ellen, "I have a meeting at five today. I probably won't be home until after seven. But no worries. Pete will be here at ten and Andrew is working from home today. So there will always be someone here if you need anything."

Ellen glanced at Andrew, who still hadn't looked up since sitting in the nook. Her ace just became a lot easier to play.

"What's the meeting about?" asked Jack, his words muffled by a mouthful of pancakes.

"The bigwigs at headquarters are considering merging our bank with some community banks. I'd be overseeing the merger, so I need to be involved from the start, ensuring all standards and rules are followed."

"You mean no cheating, right?"

Carrie took another sip of coffee. "Exactly. No cheating."

"Just like Johnny Lake," Jack said.

"Who's Johnny Lake?" Ellen asked him.

"A kid in school who found a way to cheat at Imperial Assault. It's a board game we play sometimes during lunch. He's such a bonehead."

"I can relate." Ellen nodded. "I knew kids in school who cheated all the time. Cheaters never learn how to win or get what they want legitimately. They manipulate the outcome, regardless of who they hurt." She turned her gaze toward Andrew and caught a flicker of discomfort in his eyes.

Looking at Carrie, Ellen asked, "You're not like that, are you?"

Her sister met her gaze head-on. "Of course not. Did I ever cheat at games when we were kids?"

"I don't remember," Ellen replied, filling her tone with insinuation.

"Well, *I* do," Carrie replied, turning toward Jack. "And I didn't."

"What about you, Andrew?" Ellen asked. "You're not like that, right?"

"No, I'm not. And unlike your sister, I find that question offensive." Despite the tightness in his voice and the red tint suffusing his face, he continued to eat.

Carrie's high heel tapped Ellen's shin, a warning. But Ellen couldn't resist.

"Oh, the lady doth protest too much, methinks."

The loud clang as Andrew dropped his fork made everyone at the table jump. "What the fu — What the hell is wrong with you? You're in my house and you act like this?" He turned to Carrie, holding his thumb and forefinger just barely apart in front of her face. "I'm this close!"

"This close to *what?*" Ellen asked with a smirk. She nudged Jack again. "Don't worry, Jack. Daddy's just a little sensitive."

Andrew pushed against Carrie, squirming out of the nook. She slid off the bench and stood so he could go, her eyes following her husband out of the room and up the stairs. When his footsteps stopped stomping, she sat, shaking her head with closed eyes.

"Carrie, I —" Ellen tried.

"Don't!" Carrie raised her hand. "Stop! What do you have

against Andrew? Seriously, you've treated him terribly since the first day you met him. What has he ever done to you?"

Ellen couldn't help but think, *You should really be asking what has he ever done to* you? How could such an intelligent woman be so stupid, so blind to what was going on right in front of her? Did she not see the way Andrew and Scott probably doted on each other when the couples got together? Did she never look at his phone or sneak a peek at his texts? She may be respectable in business, but she's always been nosy in private. How could she not even *suspect* anything?

Ellen bit her tongue, knowing full well that speaking up would only dig her deeper. So, she focused on her pancakes, letting the syrupy bites drown out her urge to talk.

Carrie rolled her eyes. "If you're going to stay here, please show some respect. To all of us. If you can't, I'll have Mom come pick you up."

If she hadn't spent the entire night plotting her next moves, Ellen might have demanded to be taken to the train station right then. But there were tasks she had to take care of first, a plan to set in motion. Then she would leave — by car, train, or even on foot if necessary.

"I'm sorry," she lied through her teeth.

Then she looked at Jack. "And I'm sorry to you, too." Another lie.

"I promise to behave."

The lies rolled from her mouth without the slightest friction, like a runaway train hurtling toward its destination. Ellen shoveled an entire pancake into her mouth, determined not to derail before reaching her next stop.

By 9:15, Ellen and Andrew were alone in the house. Knowing what was about to happen, she yearned for the help of another pill. But Pete's words from yesterday clung to the walls of her skull: *I'll be checking the bottle again tomorrow.*

Her shoulder pulsated with a dull ache as she stood at the base of the staircase, inhaling deeply, gathering herself. When he came, Pete might let her take another pill. She hoped. It would have been six hours since her last one at 4:00 a.m. as she lay in bed staring at the ceiling. In the meantime, she had something else to do, its importance almost distracting her from the pain.

Gripping the railing, she used its support to ascend, one step at a time. By the time she reached the top of the staircase, air wasn't getting to her lungs. She sat down on the landing, shutting her eyes and cradling her throbbing shoulder, all the while drawing breaths as deep as she could.

Ellen didn't rush herself, keenly aware that she couldn't proceed with her plan until her mind was completely clear. A few more breaths and the throbbing subsided. She stood and made her way to Andrew's office. As always, the closed door shielded him, sealing him in a sanctuary from which only the staccato rhythm of keystrokes emerged.

She tapped on it. No answer. Undeterred, she tapped again, this time with a bit more force. Still silence. Frustration welled inside her. *To hell with it!* She seized the doorknob and twisted it.

"Why are you working from home?" she asked, peering into his office.

He looked up from his computer screen, handsome features creased in a scowl. "There's a reason I didn't say, 'Come in,' Ellen. Don't *ever* open a closed door in this house without permission."

"Oh, absolutely, sir!" With exaggerated flourish, she executed a soldier's salute, her arm rigidly raised in a parody of obedience and respect.

"Look, I'm working from home because I have a copy deck due tomorrow and there are too many interruptions at my office."

Although his words implied she was now one of those interruptions, she stepped into the room and settled into the chair in front of his desk.

"Ellen, I really don't have time for —"

"You might want to make time."

She almost laughed at the confusion that flashed across Andrew's face.

"What are you talking about, and who are you to —"

"Listen, Andrew," she said steadily, "I know about your boyfriend, Scotty. I know your little secret."

His face drained of color, his eyes widening with fear or disbelief. Maybe both. "What the fuck are you talking about? I know you're nuts, but I didn't think you were *this* crazy."

Just as she'd expected, he was trying to deflect. She pressed on, undeterred. "Have you deleted the photos on your phone yet? Or are they still there so we can show Carrie together?"

Andrew stood up. Then he sat down again.

He cleared his throat and leaned back in his chair. "How would you know what is or isn't on my phone?" Even as he tried to gain control of the situation, he stammered over his words. "Are you snooping around here while we're gone? Or while we're asleep?"

"That's not important, is it?" she replied. "So, are you saying there *are* or *aren't* photos on your phone that you don't want Carrie to see?"

Andrew passed a hand over his sweat-damp forehead and

then ran it through his hair, doing nothing for his composure. He finally asked, "What are you doing? Why are you doing this? What do you want, Ellen?"

Ellen leaned back in the chair, trying to project serene confidence. The gesture caused a stab of pain through her shoulder. She grit her teeth, refusing to let him see her suffer.

"I don't want to have to tell Carrie, but she's my sister. So, you know, I really can't keep this kind of thing from her. Unless..." She left him hanging on her words.

He leaned forward and placed his elbows on the desk. "Unless what?"

"You have to do two things. First, tell me I'm right. Tell me you and Scotty Boy have something going on. Believe me, I'm not a homophobe. Not in the least. I just hate liars. So, spill the beans and you're halfway to keeping me from spilling the whole damn truth to Carrie."

Andrew covered his face with his hands. He swept his palms across his cheeks and sighed. "Even if you're right, you don't have proof. Any photos that were once on my phone are gone. You'll just be spewing shit that Carrie won't believe because she knows you're a lunatic."

Ellen cackled. "Oh, Andrew. Do you really think I'm *that* stupid? You think I wouldn't take photos of those texts as proof?"

"Fuck," he whispered. "I knew there was a reason I despised you from the second I saw you."

"You mean it wasn't my good looks?" she asked mockingly.

"Okay. Okay. You're right."

"Right about what?" she pressed, keeping her gaze on him even though he was not a pretty sight at the moment. Like pinning a bug in a collection.

"About Scott. Okay? I'm going to stop it, anyway. Are you happy?"

"I'm happy you told me the truth." A hint of relief slipped into her voice, but it also spread through her throbbing shoulder as some of her tension drained.

"Now, what else do I have to do so Carrie won't find out?"

Ellen rose from her seat and moved toward the door. He made a sound, anxious, frustrated, even despairing. Halfway there, she turned back to face him, her eyes locking with his. "You have to fuck me," she said, as steadily as ever, but softer, too, projecting a velvety touch of vulnerability. "Since Carrie won't be home till late and Jack has rehearsal, we can do it at five o'clock."

"What?" His eyes grew even wider. "Why the hell would you make me do that? You're all pissed that I'm doing something behind your sister's back, and now you want me to screw *you*, her own sister? Why?"

"Isn't it obvious?" she asked in a voice dripping with irony. "Look at me. Look at this face, this body. I've never been fucked. So I have two options. I can either pay a whore to suffer through it, but I don't have the money for that. Or I can blackmail someone. And guess what? *You're* that someone."

As Andrew grappled with his choices, he looked so confused and miserable that she could almost feel pity or concern for him. Almost. If he were a different man. "And if I don't do it?" he asked.

A smile played across Ellen's chapped lips. "Then Carrie will know her husband's having an affair, and Jack will see what a miserable, selfish liar his father really is. Your family will fall apart."

"I'm not gay...I'm..."

"Bisexual. Yeah, yeah, I know. If nitpicking the language gets you through the night, Andrew."

Glancing at the clock on the wall, she smirked again. "Tick-tock. Better figure out what you're gonna do." She walked into the hallway, but again turned around, centering herself in Andrew's office door.

She blew him a kiss. "See you at five, my love."

With a trembling hand, Andrew reached for his phone. His fingers fumbled as he tapped Scott's photo icon. He needed to speak with the only person who could understand.

"Well, hi there," Scott said when he picked up, the words tinged with flirtation.

"Cut it out," Andrew snapped. "You won't believe what's happening."

"Whoa. Slow down. Tell me what the hell is going on."

"Somehow Ellen saw your pics on my phone," he started, his voice hoarse from the fear and anger tightening his vocal cords.

"How the hell —"

"I don't know. All I know is that she took her own photos of your pics and is using them to hold me hostage."

"What do you mean, 'hold you hostage'?" Scott almost whispered. Were Jamie or Bonnie in the room with him?

"She's threatening to show Carrie the pics. To tell her about...about you and me."

"Holy shit. That little —"

"It gets worse."

"How can it get any worse?"

"She's going to tell Carrie and try to ruin our lives unless I..." He couldn't make himself say it.

"Unless you what, Andrew?" He didn't recognize the tone in Scott's voice until now. Concern for him? Hope, that Andrew might negotiate with Ellen and keep this from ruining all their lives? "What does she want you to do?"

He held his head in his open hand, still on the edge of hope that this was all a terrible dream.

"Fuck her," he said.

"What?"

"Fuck her!" He spat the words but couldn't get any volume behind them. "If I have sex with her, she said she won't tell Carrie about you and me."

A few seconds of silence passed before Scott said, "I don't get it. Why would you having sex with her stop her from telling Carrie the truth? I mean, how can you trust that once you screw her, she won't go and tell Carrie anyway?"

He wasn't about to go into the 'Chubsy Ubsy' blackmail fiasco and how this lunatic *could* be trusted, as long as her requests were met. *Twice,* he thought. *How could I let her do this to me twice?*

"What are my options, Scott? I either do it and hope she never says anything or I don't do it and know for certain she'll open her mouth. Really, what choice do I have?"

"Oh my God," Scott said. "That woman is completely out of her mind."

The knot deep in his stomach tightened. "Yeah, well, that's a given. What the hell am I supposed to do?"

"When is this supposed to happen? I mean, that aide guy is there during the day, then Carrie comes home from work and —"

"Things seem to be working out just *perfectly* for Ellen today. The aide leaves around three or four. Carrie's working late and Jack's rehearsing until six. She wants it to happen at five o'clock."

Scott let out a long, thick sigh. "This is sick. You know that, right?"

"I know it's sick. It's like something from a horror movie. She's holding all the cards right now."

"We can't let this happen, Andrew. You have to do whatever it takes. If we're exposed, our families will suffer. I was such an idiot for sending those damn pictures. I thought your lock screen had a secure code."

"Obviously, it wasn't secure enough," he retorted sharply.

Scott had a point. The secret they shared was heavy enough to crush them both and their families, too. But Andrew couldn't imagine himself being capable of what Ellen demanded. The mere sight of her repulsed him.

"How the hell can I go through with this? Just the thought of touching her makes me sick. How...how am I even supposed to...perform?"

Scott cleared his throat. "I won't sugarcoat this. You *have* to find a way. Have a few drinks, close your eyes and think of... anything that can get you through this. Think about us together. You and Carrie together. Maybe *that's* what you need to hold onto while it's happening — how saving your family will all be worth it."

"I can't understand how this rotten witch ended up pulling the strings," he muttered, resentment as bitter as ashes in his mouth.

"Don't even try to figure it out, Andrew. When you're dealing with someone like that, there's no logic. Nothing makes sense."

"Honestly, the best thing that could've happened when she fell down those steps was if she —"

"Don't go there," Scott cautioned. "We just have to fix this...*without* you going to prison, for God's sake. I wish there was something I could do to help. I *really* do. I feel useless."

"Just being able to talk with you is helping. I'm just not sure how I'm going to get through it...or even if I'll get hard enough to —"

"You *will*, Andrew. I *know* you will. A few drinks will help you not focus on what's going on. Do you need me to send you some pics?" Scott asked with total sincerity.

The knot in Andrew's stomach had tightened into a hard stone. "You're kidding me, right? That's what got me in this mess to begin with."

"I'm sorry. I just thought —"

Andrew heard the front door close and voices downstairs.

"The aide must be here. I gotta go. Maybe I should start drinking now."

"Whatever it takes, man. Whatever it takes. I'm here all day if you need to talk."

"Thank you," Andrew said, swallowing hard to hold back tears.

With those words, they both hung up.

In the silence of his office, Andrew couldn't help but think about how he got here. Not just the sticky web Ellen spun around him, but the life that included them both in the first place. Regret gnawed at his insides as he thought about the path he could have taken if he hadn't gotten married in the first place. The freedom he could have tasted, the life he could have lived. But then, he reminded himself, Jack wouldn't exist in this world.

It was Jack, the thought of his son, that offered a flicker of light against the night that loomed ahead. He would not endure this ordeal to rescue himself, or spare Carrie, or protect Scott, and certainly not to satisfy his fucking sister-in-law.

He'd do it for Jack.

CHAPTER TEN

As Andrew took a sip of scotch, his hand trembled ever so slightly, the glass clinking against his teeth. On the other end of the phone, Carrie's questioning continued.

"Do you think you'll be able to deal with her alone tonight? If not, I'll figure out a way to get home earlier and —"

"No." Andrew took another sip of alcohol, feeling its sting course through his veins. "There's no need for you to come home. I can handle her." He glanced at the clock on the wall, its ticking hands a relentless reminder of the depravity that awaited him. It was 4:50 and a wave of nausea churned in his gut. "I'll just heat some pot roast and she can eat in the living room. I'll eat in my office. I have work to do, anyway."

Carrie's voice held a hint of guilt as she asked, "Are you sure? You don't sound okay with this, and I don't want to leave you alone with her if it's going to be too much."

"Yes, I'm sure," he replied, even though he wasn't. "Don't worry. I'll manage."

For a moment the only sound was the distant murmur of voices on Carrie's end of the line.

"The meeting is starting," she said. "Andrew, tomorrow is her last day with us and then she'll be gone. I promise. One way or another, she'll be on her way home by Saturday. I know it's been rough on you."

Rough? If you only knew, Carrie.

"It's okay," Andrew murmured, his mind focused on what lay ahead of him. "It'll be fine."

"Are you sure you're okay? You don't sound like yourself. Are you feeling sick or —"

Andrew tried to clear the dread out of his throat. "I'm fine, Carrie. Fine. I just have a lot of work to do and I'm falling behind. Just focus on your meeting, and I'll see you around eight, okay?"

The voices in the background grew louder, signaling the end of their conversation. "Okay," she said. "See you around eight. Good luck with dinner."

Andrew's gaze drifted toward the ceiling, his eyes welling with both the sting of alcohol and overwhelming emotion. "Thanks." Hoping it might pass for a joke, he added, "I'm going to need it. Bye."

"Bye, hon." She barely got the words out before she hung up and Andrew was listening to dead air.

He took another swig of scotch and slammed the glass down on his desk as it burned its way down his throat as he stared at the screen where Carrie's name had been. Although the last thing he wanted was to be reminded of the time, he forced himself to look at the clock again.

Countless thoughts raced through his mind, each one a cutting reminder of the mess that was now spiraling out of control. Should he call Carrie back, confess to her and figure out a way to live with the consequences of a broken trust that could probably never be mended? The mere thought of losing Carrie and Jack, the two pillars of his existence, crushed the breath from his lungs. Could he bear living a life of loneliness and shame? Knowing that his son would grow up with a tarnished image of his father, seeing him as a man who'd hid behind a lie for years — while the truth behind that lie would certainly find its way into his high school hallways and surround him with teenage gossip. Would Jack lose friends over it as they distanced themselves from his messed-up story? Would his son wind up as lonely as Andrew himself?

"No," he whispered to the empty room, his voice held together with a fragile thread of resolve. "Just get it over with. Save your family, save your life."

He grabbed the bottle of scotch and the muffled rush of liquid cascading into the glass brought him the slightest sense of calm. Holding the glass to his lips, Andrew rose from his desk chair and left his office behind, his steps weighted with a leaden weariness. He trudged down the hallway toward the guest bedroom. With each step, he begged the universe for an escape, any loophole that might get him out of this nightmarish ordeal. But there was no response other than the scotch in his hand promising some respite, at least. He took another swig.

When he reached the guest room, he lingered at the threshold, peering inside. Tightly drawn shades cut the room off from the outside world. A feeble glow from the lamp on the nightstand between two beds seemed to intensify the shadows more than it offered any illumination.

A figure materialized in the murk — a silhouette on the edge of the bed closest to the window. Ellen sat there, wearing sweatpants and a flannel shirt. Just making out that much of her sent a chill up his neck. He placed his glass on the nightstand and reached for the lamp's switch, dimming the light to its lowest setting. As if not being able to see it would lessen the reality of what was about to happen. The entire room became indistinct, muddy, like the cloudy muck inside him.

An idea came to him, then, of how to at least delay the inevitable. He came to stand before Ellen and asked, his voice barely a whisper, but full of as much pretend concern as he could muster, "Won't this hurt?"

His words must have struck a nerve because her posture in the darkness grew more rigid. "Why would it hurt?" she snapped. "Cause I never did this before?"

Tension crackled in the air between them.

"You think I've never had anything else inside me?" she asked.

"No, Ellen," he replied, still speaking gently, as if he felt compassion for her. "I meant your shoulder. Won't this hurt?"

Ellen dismissed his feigned interest with a wave. "Don't you worry about that. And stop trying to put this off. We don't have a lot of time."

Andrew wished he hadn't left his scotch on the nightstand. Another gulp would further numb his nerves. Mustering his courage without it, he looked her in the face. What he saw made his heart skip a beat. The play of faint lamplight highlighted the skeletal contours of Ellen's face. Gaunt cheeks sank as if any remnants of flesh had been carved away. She was never attractive, but here she looked ghastly — tortured, starved. Her deep-set eyes, sunk in shadowed sockets, bore into him.

"Why are you doing this?" Andrew couldn't help but ask.

"We can't stand each other. Why make me do this? Of all people."

Ellen laughed so viciously that she fell back on the bed. He had an instant's urge to leave her there, maybe even to hit her to keep her down so she wouldn't follow him. Then she abruptly sat back up. "Oh, Andrew. You really are funny...in your own way. Foolish, but you do amuse me. To be honest, there are actually *two* reasons I'm doing this. I already told you the first one. I've never had a man inside me and want to know what it's like before I die. Who knows? I could be hit by a bus tomorrow."

Andrew let out a sigh. "Yeah, I know. I heard that one already. But what if I paid for a professional? I'll give you the money. This way it doesn't have to be me. You know...so it doesn't have to be someone you hate so much."

"That's exactly why I want it to be you," she said, her inflection dripping with malice. "I hate you and I *know* how much you've always hated me. Making you do this brings me pleasure. You don't deny yourself pleasure with Scotty, right? Why should I deny myself the pleasure I get by doing this to you?"

In a trembling voice, he said, "There's something deeply wrong with you. You know that, right?"

"Duh, Andrew. There always has been and always will be."

She pressed her hand against his crotch, but Andrew found himself unable to respond. He didn't move, not even a wince.

How the hell did he get himself into this?

Did it really matter? He was where he was, and it was his time to pay for giving in to the feelings, the urges he'd known he should suppress. This was his punishment, he assumed, for not having the strength to fight his demon.

He reached for the condom tucked in his pocket. His hands fumbled with the package.

"What are you doing?" Ellen's voice cut through the air.

"Condom," he muttered.

"No need for that," she said, almost vindictively. "I have endo-something-me-osis. Years ago it fucked up my tubes. No kids for me." Ellen snickered. "I guess that's a good thing, for you *and* the world, right?"

Andrew knew better than to answer that, so he stood silent, fingers playing over the condom package.

"And you don't have to worry about STDs or anything like that because..." Her yellow teeth appeared against her chapped lips as she smirked. "You'll be the first."

He let the condom slip from his grasp back into his pocket. With quivering hands, he unbuckled his belt, then pulled the button on his pants free from its hole. The fabric around his waist surrendered, sliding down his legs to the floor. He closed his eyes and slid his underwear below his knees. As he bent, a bead of sweat trickled down his back. The room was sweltering even with the bitterly cold March weather. It could've been the middle of summer with an air conditioner that had stopped working. Did he have a fever? Was the alcohol fueling his body heat? It couldn't be arousal.

"Thatta boy," Ellen whispered, her voice both mocking and eager. "Come closer, so I can see it."

Andrew glanced toward the nightstand, the scotch glass there, then lunged toward it and emptied the amber contents into his parched mouth.

"That's right," she said. "Do whatever it takes. Now get on top of me. I'm ready for you." The mockery had faded; now her voice trembled with anticipation.

He stood over her again and saw her pale, bony hips, a stark contrast to Carrie's soft curves. They looked almost translucent, brittle, frail enough that Andrew could imagine them cracking beneath his weight. He knew if he continued to look at her, he'd never be able to follow through on her demand.

So he closed his eyes again. His body moved mechanically in a fog of alcohol and disbelief that tainted his senses. Ellen's voice served as his guide, her sarcastic encouragements reverberating in his head. Andrew surrendered, suppressing his revulsion by forcing his mind to empty, to drain itself of all thought. No people, no desires, no dreams. Nothing. Just robotic motions that would satisfy the demon so it would allow its prisoner to escape.

When it was over, Andrew staggered back, away from the bed. Oblivious to the world around him, he pulled up his underwear and trousers and let his feet lead him toward the door. At some point going down the hallway, he became aware of where he was: on the second floor of his own home. He could have a shower in the en suite of his bedroom.

"That did not happen," he whispered to himself, his voice a faint echo against the rush of running water. "That did not just happen."

But the stream falling from the rain shower head and down his naked body couldn't wash the truth out of his flesh, or his soul. Somewhere deep down, in the darkest corners of his being, Andrew knew the stain of this encounter would haunt him until his last breath.

CHAPTER ELEVEN

Carrie stepped into the dimly lit guest room to find Ellen with her phone in one hand and a half-filled vodka tumbler in the other.

The disheveled space probably mirrored the chaos filling Ellen's head most of the day. Both beds were unmade, sheets strewn about, pants lay on the floor, and an open travel bag sat atop the dresser. On the nightstand was an empty glass with the thinnest layer of amber at its bottom.

Jesus, vodka, Vicodin and *scotch? What the hell am I supposed to do with her?*

She took a deep breath and approached her sister. "Have you eaten dinner? What have you been up to?" After a day of endless meetings, the surge of concern she felt wasn't enough to add much strength to her voice.

Ellen shrugged, her eyes on the phone screen, avoiding contact with Carrie's. "Just finished some cereal. Andrew was too busy or something. Doesn't matter. I'm fine."

Carrie looked between the half-filled tumbler in Ellen's hand and the empty glass on the nightstand. She struggled with whether or not to broach the topic now or wait until she had more energy. Deep down, she knew it didn't matter. Day or night, morning or evening, they'd end up fighting.

"Ellen, I'm really worried about your drinking," she started, pointing to the vodka. "And what was that?" She nodded to the nightstand. "Scotch?"

Ellen didn't answer.

"And you're on Vicodin. Mixing alcohol and medication is very dangerous. You're putting your life at risk. Do you realize that?"

"Oh, spare me the lecture, Carrie. I don't need your concern. I know what I'm doing." Ellen's voice dripped with both defiance and resentment.

Carrie pinched the bridge of her nose, having nothing left but a sigh and a shake of her head. "I'm not trying to lecture you. I just don't want to see you destroying yourself."

Ellen's eyes narrowed, a flash of contempt shrouding her face. "Well, lucky for you, you won't have to deal with me much longer. One more day and I'll be out of your hair. I'm leaving on Saturday."

"I didn't say anything about leaving," she said, trying not to show her relief. "I was just voicing my concern."

"I hear your concern, Carrie. It's so...so *heartfelt*."

Ellen's sarcasm struck like a hammer on Carrie's chest. It was time to change the subject.

"I really wish you and Andrew got along better," Carrie said with genuine regret. "It would've been nice if you could have spent some time together, maybe watched a movie or something. I feel bad seeing you sitting up here all alone in this room."

"Can't help you there." Ellen finally looked up from her phone and met Carrie's eyes. "He's hated me since the first day we met. And to be honest, which I always am, I don't feel much different about him. It's chemistry, I guess. Bad chemistry." She glanced toward her bedroom door. "Speaking of Andrew, where the hell is he? I haven't seen or heard him for hours."

Carrie pulled the clip from her bun, letting her hair fall on her shoulders. "He's resting. He told me he was feeling sick. I gave him some Tylenol. He said he couldn't even stomach dinner."

Something shifted in Ellen's expression, a flicker of — what? Sympathy? Regret?

Gently, Carrie asked, "Do *you* feel okay?"

Ellen took a few moments to answer, and when she did, her voice was stern, as if the question had offended her. "I feel fine. I'm gonna call Mom and tell her I'm coming home on Saturday. Especially if Andrew's sick. I've got enough pain without catching whatever he has on top of it."

"You sure about that?" Carrie asked even as the relief grew in her entire body, so strong she wanted to lie down. "You know you're welcome to stay as long as you need. I'll make sure Andrew stays away from you while he's sick and —"

"No, it's best if I go home. Mom can help me find a new doctor. We'll send over all the medical records, X-rays, surgery notes, all that shit. I need to get home. I can't stay here forever."

The torrent of Carrie's relief mingled with an undercurrent of unease. It would be great to have Ellen off her hands, but she knew their mom wasn't able to handle her either. And then what would happen? What mess would she get into next?

And yet, the unease was soon swallowed by the feeling of freedom. Followed by a flood of sadness as she realized she didn't care anymore. Maybe she was too tired. Or bitter. Or sick of the irritation caused by someone who didn't care about herself, let alone those around her. The reason didn't matter, didn't change how empty she felt.

Still, she couldn't let Ellen go without some protest. "No, you can't stay here forever, but I want to be sure you're getting whatever help you need. Believe it or not, we're all here for you. Even Andrew. "

Ellen cast a sidelong glance, her thin lips pulling in a smirk. It was eerie. "You have no idea," she murmured.

Carrie stood. "What do you mean?" Her heart pounded, her relief evaporating. What was her sister up to?

Ellen's smirk changed, turned sweeter — by Ellen's standards — until it was just a smile. Then Carrie wondered if she'd seen anything at all in her face, heard something odd in her voice. "You have no idea what that means to me." She returned her gaze to her phone. "That's all I meant."

The room descended into silence, heavy with the weight of secrets and a relationship so broken, Carrie recognized it was impossible to put the pieces back together. With a nod, she acknowledged the futility of mending what was obviously irreparable. She turned and left the room, leaving Ellen to grapple with her demons and face the consequences of her choices. She had her own life to deal with, and with Ellen's departure, the burden would be lighter... a lot lighter.

———

Ellen paced in the guest room, clutching the phone tightly. Her words, announcing her decision to return home on Saturday, seemed to hang in the room as she awaited her mother's response.

"What happened, Ellen? Why do you want to come home so soon? Something doesn't add up."

The accusation left her on edge, exposed and vulnerable. Ellen's heart raced. Although most of the alcohol's effects had relented, the opioids still had her a bit woozy. She fought to keep her voice steady. "Mom, please, I just realized I need to be home. It's been tough here. I miss my space. Why can't you understand?"

"It's not that simple, Ellen. Carrie said it was best for you to stay with them and told me that you didn't have a problem with it. And now this sudden turnaround. I'm sorry, but it's hard not to be suspicious."

"Oh my God, Mom! I changed my mind, okay? Can't people do that without being interrogated? Unless you don't want me to come home."

After a few seconds of silence, Michelle told her softly, "Don't *ever* say something like that. Of course I want you home. I just want to make sure your doctor thinks it's okay for you to make the trip."

Another pause followed. Ellen wondered if it was because of a different concern or increasing suspicion.

"Is Carrie really okay with this? I want to speak to her. I need to be sure everyone's on the same page."

Ellen's grip on the phone tightened, her mind scrambling to find the words that would allay her mother's worries. "Carrie is fine with it, Mom. We've talked about it, and she understands. I just want to be back in my own room, in familiar surroundings. I can't stand being away from home anymore."

Michelle relented, though Ellen thought she sensed

reluctance in her voice, in the hesitations between her words. "Alright, I'll start looking for a reputable orthopedist in our area. We'll get all your medical information from Dr. Waites. Just let me know if you want me to drive and come get you or if you'll be taking the train."

Ellen's eyes wandered to the window, her mind already on the journey ahead. She longed for time alone on the train, the landscape whirring by as the rhythmic clack of the wheels on the track calmed her restless and bitter thoughts. "I'll be taking the train to 30th Street Station, same place you dropped me off. As soon as I get the details, I'll let you know, okay?"

"Yes. Fine. You're sure you're ready?" Michelle asked.

Ellen nodded, though her mother couldn't see it. Her determination solidified. "Absolutely, I am *so* ready. We'll talk about it when I get home."

"Talk about what?"

Realizing she had almost revealed too much, Ellen shifted gears. "Nothing to worry about, Mom. I just want to come home. I'll call you tomorrow with the arrival time. Bye."

Ellen hung up before she could hear her mother say goodbye. As she stood in the center of the room, peering out the window at the leafless weeping willow, a whirlwind of questions tore through her mind.

Would she tell her mother *anything* about what happened during her stay? How Carrie and Andrew weren't always the lovebirds they appeared to be. How Andrew was screwing around with a man... Carrie's friend's husband, no less? That she had her first sexual experience? And how? The sad truth about Jack growing up among webs of lies, one hanging in every corner of their house?

No, she couldn't say a word. If she did, too many worlds

would explode. Her mother would probably throw her out and accuse her of ruining a young boy's life only so she could feel better about herself.

*Even I *can't do that,* she thought.

Or can I?

CHAPTER TWELVE

Carrie, Ellen, and Jack sat around the dinner table. The clinking of forks against plates filled the silence, and the spaghetti and meatballs smelled delicious, but an unspoken tension hung in the air as there had been from the day Ellen came to visit.

Jack sat across from her, his eyes darting back and forth between her and Carrie. It was as if he could sense the undercurrents of agitation swirling around them. She'd gathered that the poor kid had been a nervous wreck growing up, and Carrie worried that he still was, but just because you were a nervous wreck didn't mean everything wasn't about to go horribly wrong.

Finally she couldn't stand the quiet anymore and decided to break it.

"Where's Andrew?" Ellen asked.

"He has a big presentation tomorrow." Carrie sounded

perturbed, as if Ellen had interrupted a stream of thought. It couldn't have been a pleasant one. "The team is working late."

"Oh, like wife, like husband." Ellen was the only one to laugh at her joke. *Guess that didn't work.*

Still, even as the uncomfortable air in the kitchen grew, Ellen couldn't help but feel a surge of satisfaction at knowing that Andrew was intentionally avoiding her. The thought of his distress brought a wicked sense of triumph, a victory in their subtle warfare. And beneath the satisfaction was a flicker of disappointment. She'd hoped to rub it in his face one last time before her departure, to look in his eyes and see his humiliation and cowardice. But her disappointment was tempered by the realization that Andrew's absence was a testament to his dread. That he would go to such lengths to avoid her only made her feel more vindicated. Oh, how she relished the thought of him stewing in his own discomfort, knowing she had gotten under his skin... and a lot more.

And so now Ellen found a strange solace in the silent tension. She held a special power over this family, the potential to completely, and easily, disrupt their carefully constructed dynamic. She glanced at Jack and Carrie, a smile playing at the corners of her lips, knowing that her impact would remain within the walls of this house long after she'd left.

Carrie's phone, resting on the table, buzzed. Ellen's eyes caught Andrew's name on the screen as her sister grabbed the phone.

"I have to take this," she said, walking out of the kitchen and into the living room.

Ellen looked at Jack, who shrugged and sucked a few strands of spaghetti into his mouth.

That was when she realized, aside from the back and forth

they enjoyed while playing video games, they had never truly conversed about his life outside the house. They'd talked about journaling and his night terrors, but never about school, friends, or the play in which he starred. Just because his parents were morons, didn't mean she couldn't engage in a civil conversation with her nephew. Of course, it all depended on whether he thought she was a lunatic.

"You know, I probably watched *West Side Story* ten times on television," she said. "Your performance was just as good…if not better. Do you have a favorite part?"

Jack swallowed his spaghetti and washed it down with a gulp of water. "Actually, I loved singing 'Somewhere' while Tony's dying."

Ellen smiled, a bit surprised. She'd expected his passion to be in the dance scenes, since he was so good at it. "Why?"

"Well, it's really the line that says, *'Peace and quiet and open air wait for us somewhere.'*"

"Why *that* line?"

As Jack twirled more spaghetti onto his fork, his gaze drifted toward the sliding glass door leading into the backyard. His mind, Ellen guessed, was drifting to the stage where he had sung those dying words.

As he snapped back to the present, still holding the fork in mid-air, he turned to Ellen.

"Well, it makes me think of Heaven. You know, a peaceful place that's quiet, with a sky that goes on forever. And the best part is the way the song uses the word *somewhere*. It's not a physical place, it's like a living thing, sort of a spirit, and he's begging it to wait for them, for when they're finally together again."

"Holy shit." Ellen slapped a hand over her mouth. "Sorry I

cursed, but you seem a lot older than fifteen. I could never use my imagination for stuff like that and I'm more than twenty years older than you."

Jack shrugged again and stuffed the ball of pasta in his mouth.

Ellen was on the verge of asking him if he had feelings for the girl who played Maria, possibly more than just friendship, but Carrie returned to the kitchen in a huff. She slid her phone onto the kitchen island and resumed her seat at the table, her face flushed.

"Something wrong?" asked Ellen.

"He'll be later than expected. Lots of work still to get done."

Ellen laughed silently to herself. Was he *really* engrossed in work or was he with Scotty Boy, crying over the horror of having sex with his repulsive sister-in-law? To be a fly on the wall... or in that hotel bed... or wherever the two of them —

"What were you two talking about?" Carrie interrupted her thoughts, slicing a chunk off the cooled meatball on her plate.

"My play," Jack replied.

"Some kid you got here," Ellen remarked before taking another sip of vodka.

"Don't I know it," Carrie said before pecking Jack's forehead with a kiss. Then she turned to Ellen, the frown lines between her eyebrows deepening. She placed her fork on her plate and dabbed her mouth with the cloth napkin.

"I have to ask —" Carrie took a sip of Chianti. It seemed to give her the courage to continue, "Did anything happen between you and Andrew yesterday?"

"What are you talking about?" Ellen reached for her own glass of vodka.

"I don't know. He was just acting strange yesterday, and also this morning. Remember how he was sick when I got home last night?"

Ellen nodded, bringing a forkful of pasta to her lips.

"Well, after his nap, he said he was feeling better, but he also told me he had to be out early this morning and wouldn't be back until later tonight. He was up and dressed before I even got out of bed. Didn't even have breakfast. It was like he couldn't get out of the house fast enough."

Ellen slurped her spaghetti and swallowed. "Well, I've been in this house for a few days and can tell you, I can't wait to get out either." As the lines on Carrie's face twisted into a scowl, she backtracked. "I'm not saying it's you or this kid." She reached across the table to tousle Jack's hair. "I'm saying that he worked from home yesterday and being cooped up can make you want to run for the hills...or at least the office."

Carrie's expression softened. "I hear you. The thing is, when I told him how much I wished you two got along better, that you could've actually kept each other company last night, he seemed really irritated. It was like he was upset with you about something." She twirled spaghetti around her fork. "Angrier than usual, I should say."

"Hey, I can't help you with that," Ellen said. "You know as well as I do that Andrew and I have never gotten along." She glanced at Jack. "Should we really be talking about this in front of Jack?"

"I'm not a five-year-old," he said.

Carrie reached over and gently touched his hand. "Exactly right," she said. "You're old enough to hear this conversation. And old enough to know why I always say we don't keep anything from each other in this house."

Yeah, right. Have you checked out the pics on your husband's phone?

"Andrew and I have tried to instill in Jack the importance of our family and that no matter what, the three of us need to do whatever it takes to stay together. We're like a tripod with a fragile bowl on top. We need to stay by each other's side and remain sturdy so the bowl doesn't fall and shatter. Right, Jack?"

It was like listening to a broken record, a worn-out mantra that grated on Ellen's nerves. She wondered how long this delicate relationship with her sister could be sustained.

Jack struggled to swallow an oversized bite of meatball before responding. "Yup, if one leg falls or crumbles, the tripod falls over and the bowl breaks into a million pieces."

The metaphor hung in the air, obviously a desperate attempt by two people to preserve the illusion of unity within what Ellen knew was a fractured family. But Jack's voice had been strong and confident — the brainwashing obviously had taken hold.

You have to be kidding me with this shit.

"Oh," Ellen said, "like the way *our* family stuck together?"

"Ellen —" Carrie tried to interject.

But she refused to be silenced. She continued, her gaze shifting toward Jack.

"*We* started off with a table, four legs for mother, father, sister, and sister. But the father leg was always a bit wobbly, weak in the knees, pretty much because he was always drunk. That's what kept the other three legs on edge, waiting for the unavoidable collapse. And then, the mother leg couldn't bear the uncertainty any longer, so it kicked the father leg out. And just like that, we became a tripod...like *your* family."

Again Carrie tried to interrupt her, but Ellen pressed on, determined. "Don't you want Jack to know what happens when a tripod collapses?"

"Ellen!"

Carrie's plea hung in the overcharged atmosphere alongside the question. It went ungranted. Ellen had reached her breaking point, no longer willing to play along with Carrie's charade of unity. Her frustrations and resentments spilled like filthy river water rushing over a broken dam.

"Well, Jack, with *our* tripod, the first leg to go was the ugly, skinny one. That's me. We all knew it would go first because it was the weakest — physically and mentally. That leg just couldn't get its shit together. The other two watched it crumble and didn't really do much to help hold it up. Yeah, they put some tape on it, a little glue here and there, but then a crack would show up somewhere else. So while that leg wobbled and tried to stay standing, the stronger leg — the pretty, popular and smart leg — pulled herself away from the other two legs. Geez, what a mess *that* was. It was like the tripod was straddling one of those cracks in the ground when an earthquake hits."

"Ellen! Enough!" Carrie yelled.

"Wait, I didn't get to the oldest leg yet. The mother leg...the one that loved the pretty, popular, smart leg, but was cursed with the weak one...the leg that could barely stand at all. In the end, each of the three legs was really on their own. Like splinters of a tree after it's been struck by lightning. Thrown to the ground. Twigs, just stuck in the dirt, never in contact with each other again except when the sun hits them from a certain angle and their shadows meet."

Jack's mouth hung open; his fork hadn't moved since she'd started her monologue. When she finished speaking, he looked at Carrie. Ellen did too, taking the sight of mascara running down her cheeks.

Carrie tapped his hand in a silent plea. After wiping her face with her napkin, she turned to Ellen, her pitiful expression overtaken by one of disdain.

"That is the exact opposite of what we're trying to teach Jack. Maybe, Ellen, I took what happened with our family, learned from it and am trying to make sure it doesn't happen with mine."

More out of curiosity than anything, Ellen waited for her to continue, and continue she did.

"Blame whoever you want for our family problems. Blame me, blame Mom. Blame our father all you want. But in the end, we have to take control of our own lives and our own futures. If *you* can't get over the past, there's only one person to blame, and you'll see her whenever you look in the mirror."

Ellen laughed so hard she found herself slapping the table with her hand. When she finally got enough breath to reply, Carrie spoke first.

"We are done with this conversation. As usual, you've ruined another meal...another time we could have enjoyed being together. You just can't help yourself, can you?" She lifted her wineglass and after taking a sip, kept holding it with the obvious intention of having more. "Don't answer that. This discussion is over."

But Ellen had no intention of stopping just yet. She had one last message to deliver.

"You're a good kid, Jack," she addressed him with sincerity as a prelude to offering one of her life's most important lessons. "Tripods are important, but they're not always reliable. There's always one weak leg that'll let you down. Make sure you're standing on both of yours so when you find out which is the undependable one, you won't fall down with it."

Ellen stood up, tossing her napkin to the table. As it hit the table, she looked from Jack to Carrie's gape-mouthed faces.

Walking out of the kitchen, she rubbed her sore shoulder and said the only words left to say. "I'm going upstairs to pack."

CHAPTER THIRTEEN

Although the June sun beat down on the back of Michelle's neck, a little sweat was a small price to pay for the heat melting the memories of the cold, snowy winter. The low spring temperatures forced her to delay her typical May planting, but she was thankful for today's warmth and also that the plants she'd bought a few weeks earlier continued to thrive.

On her hands and knees, she immersed herself in the therapeutic rhythm of tending the flower beds. She'd spent the morning meticulously preparing the soil with just enough water and fertilizer to help the begonias, daffodils, marigolds, and variegated hostas she'd purchased grow quickly. It was her favorite time of year, a rebirth of sorts, when anything seemed possible, and today it was as if nature itself rejoiced in the arrival of this long-awaited season.

She breathed in the sweet scent of the potted flowers awaiting their new home in the earth surrounding her front yard. Above her, climbing hydrangeas draped their leaves across the pergola; eventually, they'd grow into a canopy of green to shade the delicate blooms below. Michelle took a deep breath as a birdsong mingled with the gentle rustle of leaves in the breeze. At that moment, she felt more at peace than she had in months, maybe even years.

Her neighbor, Janice, working in her own flower beds, sent a friendly wave across the street. Michelle waved back and, wanting to catch up with someone she hadn't talked with in months, stood and made her way over.

"What a day!" Janice said, rising and kissing Michelle on the cheek. "These knees aren't what they used to be." She looked ruefully down at the pads strapped around them.

"I hear that!" Michelle replied, pointing to her own dirty knees. "I should get a pair of those. My knees are killing me...not to mention my back, shoulders, arms, and elbows."

Janice smiled. "Getting old is wonderful, isn't it?"

"They're the golden years, I'm told."

She giggled at the sarcasm. "Golden or rusty?"

Michelle bent her head back and laughed. But a hint of weariness crept into her voice as she said, "I like that one. Rusty it is. These golden years seem to come with more rust than expected. I knew there'd be aches and pains as I got older, but I never expected them to be so...achy."

"You know, since they say laughter is the best medicine and that yoga is great for stretching the muscles, maybe we should start a laughter yoga class. We'd have people laughing and stretching at the same time. We'd be millionaires in no time!"

"Laughter yoga, huh? Well, sign me up. I could use a good laugh to ease these rusty joints of mine." The chuckles Janice got out of her were helping.

But she didn't feel like laughing much as her neighbor asked, "How's Ellen doing? Her arm? Wrist?"

"Ahhh...to be thirty-nine again. Everything heals a lot quicker when you're young. She went to physical therapy a few times. Now she does some exercises and stretching at home using online videos. It's almost like it never happened."

"Well, that's good to hear," Janice said. "When I broke my foot, I —"

Her gaze shifted, looking at something over Michelle's shoulder. She turned, following it, to see Ellen standing at the front door beckoning her with the urgency of someone summoning an engine to a house on fire.

"Mom!" she shouted.

Michelle didn't see any smoke and Ellen didn't look injured, but the sound of a frantic voice formed a knot inside her chest anyway.

And it was such a beautiful day.

"I'm sorry, Janice." For a moment, irritation and guilt had Michelle closing her eyes; she forced them to open and her lips to unpurse so she could pleasantly excuse herself from her neighbor. "I need to see what Ellen needs. Can we catch up later?"

"Absolutely," Janice replied, her smile sympathetic now. "Don't worry about it. Family comes first. Take care of whatever it is." As Michelle started across the street, Janice called after her, "Remember, Michelle, even if we're a little rusty, we still shine."

"Thanks for reminding me."

Michelle hurried to her house, trying to hold on to the expression of compassion on Janice's face. But as she thought of the reason for it — the years of challenges she'd faced with

Ellen, more burdened than buoyed by her love for her daughter — a twinge of self-pity struck her in the gut.

"No!" she muttered. She stepped up on the curb and walked across the strip of grass onto her front lawn. She thought about the conversations she'd had with the other parents in her group. *Don't pity yourself. Stand* up *for yourself.* And if whatever Ellen was about to confront her with made her angry or upset, standing up for herself was exactly what she would do.

For the first time in a very long time, she didn't hide her annoyance and impatience as she climbed the front steps.

"What's so important, Ellen?"

"I... Wh...wha..." Whatever had Ellen so upset, it made her fumble with her words. "What's that thing the doctors say I have? Endometriasis or endomatis..."

Michelle sighed. "Endometriosis, Ellen. Your memory isn't *that* bad, you know what it is. You even had laparoscopic surgery for it! And if you forgot the exact word, why wouldn't you just look it up online?" She took a breath, trying to calm herself. "Why are you asking? Are you having pain again?"

Ellen brushed off Michelle's question and continued with her own. "Didn't they say my tubes were all messed up...that I'd never have kids?"

Michelle nodded. "Yes. The damage to your fallopian tubes made it highly unlikely for you to conceive. There was scarring after the surgery." The tension in her gut spread, and with it a chill that drove away the June sun. "Why? What's going on?"

Ellen held up a pregnancy test. Michelle's heart skipped a beat even before she registered the plus sign. And registering the sight didn't mean she believed it. "What the hell is this?" Teetering, her body instinctively leaned against the outside wall beside the door for support, piloting itself without her. "Where did you get this?"

"What do you mean?" Ellen said matter-of-factly. "It's the second one I've peed on this week, and it's the second one that shows a plus sign."

Questions raced through Michelle's mind like debris inside a tornado's funnel. How this could happen? When? And with whom? Overwhelmed, she pushed past Ellen and made her way into the house. In the living room, she collapsed onto the sofa.

Ellen joined her, taking a seat on the loveseat across from Michelle. Her earlier franticness had eased; now she seemed, if anything, even calmer than usual.

Michelle continued the struggle to gather her thoughts, to make sense of the situation or at least understand Ellen's perception of it. With another deep breath, she summoned the strength to sit up straight and meet her daughter's gaze.

"Okay, let's say, hypothetically, that the doctors were wrong. Let's say that having a child *is* a possibility. Who the hell would the father be?"

"I'd rather not talk about that right now."

"You'd rather not talk about it? Are you kidding me, Ellen?" Her voice rose, anger surging through her chest and up her throat. "You hardly ever go out, and I'm rarely away from the house. Did you use some app to invite a stranger here? Did you bring someone into our home to screw you?"

Ellen laughed and rolled her eyes. "Mom, language!"

"This isn't a joke, Ellen. Who did this to you?"

"No one did this to me," she replied, still so goddamn calm. "It was consensual, and we can discuss it another time."

Michelle clenched her fists. She couldn't let this go, not when the stakes were so high; not when other lives were involved like a child and a father who might think he'll be moving in to be part of her family. She rose from the sofa and stood in front of Ellen, hands on hips.

"Do you think you can just brush this off and avoid the conversation? That's not how it works, Ellen! We're going to talk about this, right here, right now."

Ellen's eyes flashed with defiance, but tension ran through her body as she met her mother's gaze. "Fine," she spat. "What do you want to know?"

Michelle took a deep breath, attempting to rein in her emotions. She needed answers, no matter how difficult they might be to hear. "Who is the father, Ellen? I need to know."

She fumbled her words again. "Wh-what does it matter, Mom? You won't approve of whoever it is anyway. So why b-bother?"

Michelle covered her face with her hands. Eyes closed, she peered into the darkness, trying to make sense out of what Ellen was saying... or not saying. She combed her fingers through her hair and took another deep breath. She couldn't let this continue to be a shouting match. "It matters because we need to understand the situation. We need to figure out what comes next, how we're going to handle this."

"I don't want to talk about it, okay?" she said in barely a whisper, her eyes darting away from Michelle's. "It's complicated."

"Complicated or not, right now we're in this together, Ellen. I'm your mother and am here to support you. But I can't do that if you shut me out. We need to discuss this and we need to discuss it now."

Ellen stood up. "Well then, discuss it by yourself, because I don't want to talk about it."

"I'm sorry," Michelle said. "We won't talk about that right now. Let's focus on what you're going to do. I know a clinic nearby, on Filbert and South 8th Street. One of my students had to go there for an abortion. I'll call and make an appointment so we can start the —"

"What are you talking about, *abortion?*"

"What are *you* talking about? You're not considering keeping this baby, are you?"

"No, I'm not considering it. I'm knowing it. I'm going to have this baby." The vulnerability, any shadow of uncertainty, had vanished from her voice.

"Please tell me you're joking, Ellen. You can barely take care of yourself. How are you going to care for a baby?"

"I'll be able to do it. I know I can. I'm smarter than you think."

Michelle hesitated before saying another word. She wanted to convey her concerns without hurting Ellen's feelings and driving her away. Still, she knew that if she didn't address this now, the responsibility of caring for the child would ultimately fall on her.

When she did speak, though, she didn't manage to temper her own emotions. She was confused and tired and, damn it, her knees still ached from the garden work that had been interrupted. "Forget about how smart you think you are. You're lazy. You drink excessively, which could harm your liver. You're on medications that could potentially harm the baby's development. Years ago, you wanted a dog, and when we got one, you neglected him. There were days when you wouldn't even get out of bed to feed, walk, or care for him. And now you think you can handle a baby? The crying, the diapers, the sleepless nights, the constant demands —"

"Stop!"

Undeterred, Michelle said, "No. I'm not going to stop. I'm going to continue until I can get through your head the challenges and —"

"There's no need to continue because I'm not listening," Ellen said, storming up the flight of stairs.

Feeling a wet trickle on her face, Michelle wiped away the tear. "Why can't you see? I'm not saying all of this to hurt you," she shouted so Ellen could hear her from the top of the staircase. "I'm saying it because I love you. I've tried to give you what you need...to provide the best life possible for you. But there's no way I can take on the responsibility of a baby at this stage in my life."

Ellen's footsteps sounded along the second floor and then on the steps as she made her way back down. "You can't control my choices, Mom. I've made up my mind, and I'm not changing it."

Her eyes, when Michelle met them, brimmed with determination.

"I know I can't control your choices, but I can't sit back and watch you make a decision that will impact *both* our lives. We have to think about what's best for you and me as well as for a potential child."

Ellen's face twisted with anger, and resentment filled her voice as she said, "You've never understood me, you know. You've always tried to mold me into what you wanted, into someone like Carrie. But I'm not Carrie, I'm *me* and this is my life — my decision, and I won't let you make it for me."

Michelle's shoulders slumped. "I'm not trying to make your decisions for you. I just want what's best for you. I want you to have a fulfilling future filled with happiness. But raising a child when you're not ready, when you can barely take care of yourself... it's a recipe for disaster."

"A recipe for disaster?" Ellen repeated her mother's words with such anger, it sounded as though it came from somewhere else. "Why don't you look at your *other* kid? Look at *her* family. You think *that's* not a recipe for disaster?"

"What are you talking about? What's going on at Carrie's house? Why didn't you say anything until —"

"Find out on your own," Ellen retorted, turning and walking back up the stairs. "I'm too tired to talk about anything anymore. I'm done. And if you don't want me living here with my child, *your* grandchild, I'll just move out. It's that simple."

Michelle heard a few more heavy footsteps and then the slamming of Ellen's bedroom door.

"Why me?" she whispered, the weight of three worlds sitting on her shoulders. For a fleeting moment, she wished that Ellen would have the baby and it would turn out just like her. It was the only way she'd understand the pain and struggles Michelle had endured for the past thirty-nine years, the sacrifices she'd made, relinquishing her own life to help her daughter live hers.

"It'll serve you right," she muttered, longing for the tranquility and joy she'd felt in the garden only minutes before.

CHAPTER FOURTEEN

Michelle found a spot on the street to park her car right in front of her student's house. With a sigh of relief, she rolled up the windows, sealing herself off from the outside air and noises but not from the sights around her. Blossoming crape myrtle graced the sidewalks and children played on front lawns, laughing for all the world, seeming innocent and carefree.

It should have been a scene that offered Michelle solace; she should have been able to take this moment to immerse herself in the simple joys of life. But her thoughts cast a dark shadow over the beauty that surrounded her. The worry gripping her every muscle created a tension so powerful that her body and mind both felt numb.

She took her cellphone from the passenger seat and dialed Carrie's number. She held her breath, her heart pounding with anticipation as the call connected. But instead of a familiar voice, all she heard was a hollow silence.

"Carrie? Are you there?"

"Yes, sorry. I'm here. Just had to get into my office. Where are *you*?" she asked in an amused tone. "You sound like you're in a tunnel."

"I'm sitting in my car, parked right in front of Jimmy Johnson's house. You know, the kid I tutor in algebra."

"Jimmy Johnson? Seriously? That's his actual name?"

Michelle, however, was in no mood for joking around. "Yes, that's his real name."

"Why are you calling from your car? You never —"

"I needed privacy."

"Uh oh, what happened?"

She took a deep breath before delivering the news. "You are not going to believe this, but Ellen's pregnant."

As the silence stretched out, Michelle pressed the phone against her ear. "Are you there?" she asked, her throat tight with apprehension. "Did you hear me?"

"Yes, I'm trying to process what you just told me. First of all, who —"

"Don't even bother asking about the father. She won't tell me a thing."

"Mom, she goes nowhere, doesn't do anything. I don't get it. How the hell could she get pregnant?"

Michelle fought back tears as she struggled to make sense of it all. "I've been racking my brain trying to figure it out since she told me. The only thing I can think of is those hookup apps, you know? Meeting strangers for casual encounters. She must be meeting them before or after her therapy sessions, or maybe they come to the house while I'm at my parents' group or at tutoring sessions. God knows how many she's been with." Overwhelmed, she pressed her fingers against her temples, as if that could ward off the sickening thoughts racing through her head. "I can't even bear to think about it. It makes my stomach churn."

She listened to Carrie struggling to find words. At last: "Mom, don't jump to conclusions. You don't know that's the case. Maybe she's been seeing someone long-term...someone you don't know about."

"C'mon, Carrie. You know her life. She doesn't have one. And what insignificant life she *does* have, I know just about everything that goes on in it." She paused and closed her eyes. "Well, at least I *thought* I did."

"I...I literally don't know what to say. We need to find out how this happened. In the meantime, how far along is she? Have you made plans to help her terminate the pregnancy?"

"If you think her getting pregnant is crazy, brace yourself. She actually wants to have the baby."

Another round of silence.

"Do you believe it?" Michelle didn't, herself, but it would help to know Carrie was entering this bizarre new reality with her.

"She can barely brush her own teeth. How the hell does she think she can take care of a child?"

Michelle gazed up the street, barely able to see the trees and children through the blur of tears. "You're asking me? I wish I had recorded the nights I spent with her as a baby — the endless screams and inconsolable crying. The croup, the never-ending illnesses with sleepless nights. The postpartum depression, countless diaper changes, stubborn rashes, the endless doctor visits. It was basically twenty-four-seven chaos."

Michelle appreciated Carrie's silence now. It gave her the space to vent, to get some of the weight off her shoulders. The words tumbled out in a rush. "If I had a recording of those moments, I'd play it for her, a glimpse into the realities of motherhood. But she's clueless. And she's a stubborn little brat who thinks she has it all figured out. As if she understands what being a mother is like. Sometimes I wonder why I even bother."

"I hear you, Mom. I do. I can't imagine what you're going through, but you put up with it because you *are* her mother."

Michelle's voice cracked from the emotions rising and falling within her. "When I told her there would be no baby in this house, she said she'd move out."

She heard Carrie's breath catch. "Well, she can't pay rent, and there's no way in hell she's going to live in *this* house. So where does she think she's going to go?"

"I have no clue." Michelle's brows furrowed with the confusion she'd felt from the moment Ellen uttered her threat. "I really don't know where her head is at. I'm going to do everything in my power to convince her that she simply can't have this baby. *I* can't have another child to raise. And you know it would fall on my shoulders."

"Are you going to discuss this with Dr. Blout? You know Ellen, she might not even tell her psychiatrist she's pregnant until the child is ten years old!"

Michelle sighed. "Of course, I'll bring it up. But you know how Ellen is. She's more focused on getting her meds than actually trying to work on her problems. I doubt she'll be as forthcoming as she should be."

Carrie cleared her throat. "What will you do if she keeps refusing to terminate?"

"Then she's gone. I can't take any more of this. I know she's my daughter, and I've always preached about how important it is to keep the family together, but I can only take so much. My patience ran out long ago, and I've never received an ounce of gratitude from her. Nothing. This situation is pushing me to the brink. One way or another, if she tries this, I'll get her out of my life once and for all."

Blinking away tears, Michelle checked the time. She had ten minutes before her tutoring session started. Was that enough time to get into the other thing that puzzled her? She decided to just go for it.

"There's something else," she said.

"You're joking, right? There's more?"

"I'm afraid so. During my...let's call it a *chat* with Ellen, she mentioned you. I was telling her that having this baby is a recipe for disaster. And she said something about *your* family being a recipe for disaster."

"What?" Carrie yelled. "She has no right to talk about my family, especially after what we did for her. And what is she even talking about?"

Michelle bit her knuckle. Should she ask? She and Carrie had always been open and honest about their lives and this was no time to stop.

Still, her question came out timid and awkward. "Do you...do you think she knows?"

"Knows what? What could she —" Michelle heard the slightest gasp on the other end of the phone. "Wait, you think she knows about Andrew?"

"I'm sorry, honey. That's the only possibility I can think of. Unless there's something going on with you or Jack, which I doubt."

"No," Carrie said. "There's no *way* she could know. She was here for what...a week? Nothing happened during that time. I'm certain of it. Honestly, I don't think Ellen and Andrew shared ten words with one another. And you understand how

155

sensitive that subject is. You're the only other person who knows."

Michelle wasn't sure of anything anymore. She had one infantile-acting daughter who was pregnant and wouldn't tell her who the father was. And she had another daughter who'd found out her husband was having an affair with a man and forgave him without even confronting him. She'd begged Carrie to talk with Andrew about it, to get counseling, to at least bring it out into the open. But she refused.

"It's not a big deal," Carrie said the first time she'd brought it up to her mother. Michelle wasn't sure which one of them she was trying to convince more. "It's just sex and I've known about his preferences for years, even before we got married."

"Then why would you marry him?" asked Michelle. "You're beautiful and successful. You have so many options. Why would you marry a man who would rather have sex with men?"

"It's not that he *prefers* them to me. It's just something he needs to do every now and then." Carrie tried to explain. For years she'd struggled to bring Michelle over to her way of thinking, but she'd never convinced her. "He's perfect in every other way," she'd say. "And since I don't have the highest sex drive in the world, why not have a family with the perfect man who every once in a while...?"

"Once in a while, what?" Michelle asked sharply, forcing her to put it into words.

"Fools around...has a fling. We still have sex sometimes. We have a wonderful son and a great life. This is just a blip."

"Do you have any idea who...who he...sleeps with?"

"Mostly, no, I don't. And I don't want to know. This has been going on for years, Mom. Do you think I keep a calendar of those kinds of events?" Carrie took in a deep breath and slowly exhaled. "I hear where you're coming from and I'd probably feel the same way if I were in your position. But I'm not. I'm in my position. So if you want to call it repression, call it repression. If you want to call it denial, call it denial. Whatever you want to call it, call it. If I can get past it, why can't you?"

"Because you deserve someone who doesn't sleep with other people *and* doesn't hide things from you. Why don't you even talk to him about it?"

"Mom, trust me. I've done a lot of research on bisexuality and the struggles, that for some, have to be dealt with every day for their entire life. I know Andrew. If I confronted him, if he knew that I knew, he'd be so filled with shame I'm scared he might...he could do something to himself that would not only wreck the life we've built, but would also leave Jack without a father. I can't let that happen. I *won't* let that happen."

"And you don't want to see a therapist? I'm not talking about both of you. I mean just for yourself so you have someone to talk to and get advice from."

Carrie laughed a little. "*You're* my therapist, Mom. *You're* who I talk to."

"But I'm not a professional."

"I don't need a professional to tell me I'm discrediting my worth and living a lie. This arrangement might not work for everyone, but it works for me. And right now it's working for Andrew, Jack, and the life we're living. I know it might seem nuts to you, but I won't risk any of that. It's just not worth it."

To this day, Michelle couldn't wrap her head around Carrie's mindset. She'd lived with Ben for over twelve years, a man who treated her and her children like trash. Now here was Carrie, living with a man who was lying to her, lying to himself, every single day. Was she jaded by what she'd been through with Ben?

Was Andrew just a fantastic, caring husband and co-provider with a problem Carrie had learned to live with? Or was he as bad a person as Ben?

No... he was definitely not as bad as Ben. Sure, Andrew's lying and sleeping around, but at least he's not physically abusive. He treats Jack like gold and helps provide for the family. I don't like it, but I can see why Carrie might stick with Andrew instead of taking the risk of finding another guy — maybe even a Ben.

She glanced at the dashboard clock.

"Shoot, I'm sorry, Carrie. I have one minute before this session starts. We can talk later if you want."

"It's okay, Mom." She sounded worn out, the conversation obviously taking a toll on her. "I'm sorry you're going through this. This stuff with me. This new stuff with Ellen. I'm here for you and maybe we can figure out a way for us to talk to Ellen together."

"You know, sometimes..." Michelle's voice trailed off, guilt hanging a shadow over her words.

"What, Mom? Go ahead, you can say it."

Michelle hesitated, wrestling with the turmoil inside. When she did finally speak, her voice was softened by the regret it held. "Sometimes, I don't even know why she's here."

"What do you mean?" Carrie asked.

A groan slipped past her lips. "I won't say it out loud," she murmured, "because if I do, I'm afraid God will strike me down... and you might, too."

CHAPTER FIFTEEN

E llen's quick trip downtown to get her prescriptions somehow took a turn. After waiting in line at the pharmacy for what felt like an eternity, she found herself at the huge Target down the street, surrounded by a sea of infant clothing.

The tiny garments spanned a rainbow spectrum of pastels and primary colors. Embossed with innocent motifs of animals, stars, and hearts, each one served as a potent reminder of the miracle inside her and the joy of motherhood she soon hoped to feel.

The sad fact of the matter was — and Ellen could admit it — she was more excited about the family turmoil this baby was about to create than the actual baby itself. She'd spent countless hours trying to convince herself that she would soon start to feel her maternal instinct, that unwavering connection to and love for the life inside her. So far, though, she felt nothing.

Was it because Andrew was the father? Was her loathing and indifference toward him spilling over onto the kid? Or was she just unable to feel the same affection and emotions normal women felt? Maybe her mother was right. Maybe she *was* making a mistake.

"Stop!" Ellen whispered to herself. She wouldn't allow her mother's fears and old-fashioned thinking to get in her way. Although getting pregnant was not a part of her original plan, it now played the biggest role in her new one. She would use it to her advantage, emotionally and maybe even financially.

She traced her fingers along the butter-soft fabric of the onesies. The whispering brush of cotton against her skin as the faint scent of newness delicately teased her senses triggered... something. Some emotion. Even a lot of it.

Is this the joy I'm supposed to have? Am I getting it right? Will I ever get it right?

Her eyes began darting around, sneaking glances at the other women around her. Some waddled with bellies full and round. Others weren't showing yet. Several women, like her, wandered solo, while another had a gaggle of children trailing her. Many touched the tiny clothes with a familiarity, a sign they'd done this many times before.

Ellen felt the sharp pang of envy. She was nine weeks pregnant, according to her meticulous count of days since her encounter with Andrew. Yet her stomach remained flat. She craved a round belly, visible proof she had a life growing inside her. She yearned to share her secret with the world. But there was no one else to tell, not quite yet.

She toyed with the idea of asking one or two of the women when they started to show, her mind teetering between curiosity and fear. She'd worked hard to make sure she'd never again become a Chubsy Ubsy, but pregnancy was going to change that. If she took the action her mother was pushing her to take, she'd stay thin as a rail without the worry of losing weight after giving birth. Because there'd be no birth.

That would mean continuing the monotonous cycle of her life, a life that had her questioning her very existence every morning. Having a child would answer that question while also causing the familial chaos she was so excited about. She wouldn't let the prospect of a few extra pounds stop her from having the chance to experience those feelings... whenever those pounds actually decided to appear.

Screw it, she thought, *I'll never see any of these people again.* She scanned the women in the aisles for one who was visibly pregnant and didn't have loud kids in her wake.

Her gaze settled on a petite woman sporting dark hair in a pixie cut. She held up a yellow onesie covered with tiny embroidered ducks, inspecting every stitch as if it were a Versace skirt.

Taking a deep breath, Ellen approached her and plucked a onesie off the rack. "Hi."

In response, the woman offered a quick nod and a faint, polite smile.

"Can I ask you something? It might sound a little strange. When did you start to show?" She gestured toward the woman's belly with the onesie hanger.

Caught off guard, the woman knit her eyebrows together in surprise before answering, "Around the fourth or fifth month."

A sigh of relief escaped Ellen.

"How far along are you?" the woman asked.

"About nine weeks."

"Oh, you've still got time. Enjoy it while you can," she advised, placing the yellow onesie back on the rack.

"I will," Ellen said. But she wouldn't enjoy it. Ellen knew she'd be measuring her belly every day searching for that additional half inch, then inch, then inches. She lost her patience just thinking about it.

The creases on the woman's forehead deepened as she selected another onesie from a nearby display table. In concentration, or in judgment of the strange young woman asking her personal questions? When she turned back, Ellen braced herself, awaiting an onslaught of criticism. *This is why I can't stand people. They pretend they care and then they judge me for just —*

"It's strange." The woman stepped closer so her lips were only inches from Ellen's ear. "I've always heard men find pregnant women attractive. But my husband had the exact opposite reaction. I just hope things return to normal after I give birth. That's why I advised you to enjoy your time, in case your husband reacts the same way mine did."

What a presumptuous bitch! What makes her think I have a husband? How typical. Then Ellen thought, *Eh, why not play along?*

"He doesn't know yet," she revealed.

The woman stepped back, her expression transforming into one of surprise.

Ellen added, "I only found out a day ago and plan on breaking the news in the next few days."

The woman nodded, features softening. "I don't want to pry. I mean, I don't even know your name. Is this your first child?"

"Yes."

"Why are you waiting to tell him? Are you worried about his reaction?"

"Not at all," Ellen said. "He already has a son from a previous marriage, so I'm hoping for a girl. I think he'd love to have a little princess to pamper."

"Oh, Daddy's little girl. Have you decided how you're going to tell him?"

Ellen paused, mulling over the possibilities for the story she was about to invent. This was *her* secret and she wasn't telling anyone, not even the father. But this woman had no idea what the truth was so she could spew as much bullshit as she wanted. And she did. "I'm thinking about a romantic dinner or a weekend getaway. But then, telling the whole family at once might be the way to go. We're all quite close, and I know they'd love to share in the surprise and joy with us. They'll be as shell-shocked as him. To be honest, at one point I didn't think I'd ever be able to have children. But miracles happen."

The woman nodded, a soft smile ghosting over her lips. "What a lovely story. Life really does have a way of surprising us, doesn't it?" she murmured.

Ellen chuckled, a strained sound, while her heart pounded in her chest. "You have no idea."

She let her gaze wander to the woman's belly, and her hand instinctively rose, lingering in the air for a moment. "May I?" she asked quietly.

The woman nodded, her smile faltering just a fraction.

As her palm made contact with the rounded surface, a jolt like electricity coursed through her. It was almost as though she could feel the life thriving inside. Ellen's eyes shifted back to the woman's face.

"Do you know if it's a boy or girl?" she asked, not really caring.

"A girl," the woman answered in a voice filled with a quiet pride.

"Congratulations. A little princess. I think I'll wait to find out my baby's sex. That way everyone will be more surprised...even me!"

The woman nodded, her eyes soft. "Well, whatever you decide, I hope everything turns out well for you."

"Thanks. By the way, I'm Ellen."

"I'm Carrie."

"What a coincidence. That's my sister's name!"

It's more than a coincidence, Ellen thought, *it's a sign.* This chance encounter of meeting a woman with the same name as her sister was the universe telling her that fate was part of her life-altering event. Whatever happened down the line, she didn't know, and really didn't care. Right now, this was the sign she needed to let her know she was doing the right thing, no matter what consequences lie ahead.

"Oh my, that *is* a coincidence!" the woman said. "Well, I hope Carrie will be as surprised and happy as your husband."

Ellen laughed. "She already knows. My mother told her a few days ago."

"Darn. So no surprise for Carrie then."

"Oh, no. She'll still be surprised."

Her eyebrows knit together. "Why? What's left to surprise her about?"

Ellen leaned in until her face was inches from Carrie's. "Her husband's the father."

Once she saw the shock register on Carrie's face, she pivoted on her heel and strode away. Her heart pounded with a rush of adrenaline, but she felt her lips curving into a smile that stretched across her face like a banner of triumph.

Her secret, once burdensome, now felt like a powerful weapon, and she reveled in the intoxicating feeling it gave her... even if the only person who knew the truth so far was a stranger in Target.

CHAPTER SIXTEEN

"She's pregnant."

Carrie's words hung in the living room like a foul odor, a sour note disrupting the harmony of their evening. But the news they delivered landed on him not like a vapor but like a punch to the gut. Andrew's scotch, halfway to his throat, made a hasty exit, some of it dribbling out his nostrils.

"Wha...what are you talking about? What do you mean, pregnant?"

Carrie rolled her eyes. "Uh, I think you know what 'pregnant' means. With child...expecting...in a family way."

Ellen, pregnant. Andrew's pulse thumped in his ears as a tide of panic surged. Other than him, there was no one who would...

He couldn't even complete his thought. The implications were too catastrophic. It wasn't possible. It simply couldn't be. He took another swallow of Johnnie Walker Black and placed the tumbler on the table beside the sofa.

"I don't believe it. No way. Who would even...I mean..." Andrew forced out the question, "Who is the father?"

He prayed Carrie would say a name he didn't recognize. Maybe someone Ellen had met in a supermarket, a coffee shop, or over the internet. Maybe she'd finally saved enough money to hire a professional who would have sex with her and enough extra to convince him not to use a condom. *Please, tell me it's someone else's. Please...*

With a shrug and a blank expression, Carrie said, "My mother has no clue. Ellen isn't spilling a thing. Mom's convinced she had a fling through some online hookup app. She's freaking out thinking that Ellen might have had someone come to the house and...well...you know...get her pregnant. The thought of it makes her sick and very, *very* angry."

Andrew, his throat ablaze with the remnant scotch, grasped the glass and drained it.

"Mom also told me she let Ellen know that she refuses to have a child living in the house."

"Wait, you mean she's keeping it?" The mere thought of Ellen nurturing a child, possibly his own, was unfathomable.

The breeze drifting through the open windows had changed from comfortably cool to boiling. Sweat gathered on his neck beneath a collar that suddenly felt too tight.

"Apparently yes." Carrie's voice remained flat. "She wants to keep it."

Andrew stood up so rapidly his armchair scraped against the floorboards. He moved to the bar with jerky steps and filled his glass with more scotch. When his hand shook, it sent amber liquid sloshing over the rim to stain the polished wood.

"More scotch?" A little emotion in Carrie's tone now: confusion and concern. "Why is your hand trembling like that?

You seem more shell-shocked from this Ellen thing than *I* am." His pulse throbbed in his ears again, almost blocking out her next words. "I was half expecting something drastic from her; she's been too quiet since she went home. Remember that time a few years ago when she went missing for days, only for the cops to find her drinking herself into oblivion in some hotel? But this...this is *so* beyond the pale that I still can't comprehend it."

Andrew took a deep gulp of scotch and nodded. All he wanted was to call Scott. He'd have something to say, if only *Holy shit, that bitch*. He might not solve the problem but at least he'd remind Andrew he wasn't alone in it. But he couldn't leave the room without arousing Carrie's suspicion.

He shook his head, trying to work his way back to the conversation with her. "I thought she had something wrong with her tubes years ago. Something that made it impossible for her to have kids." Andrew knew he was grasping at straws.

Carrie's eyebrows shot up in surprise. "How did you remember *that?*"

He shrugged, unable to come up with a safe answer.

"She'd been diagnosed with endometriosis. There were fallopian tube issues and doctors were skeptical about her chances of ever conceiving. Especially after her surgery, they said she would most likely never be able to have children. But it seems the 'most likely' prognosis was really just a 'maybe,' because now she has a life growing inside her." She sighed, taking a sip of her Cabernet. "Crazy, isn't it?"

"You know she's a habitual liar," he said, bitterness in his voice even as a thread of hope unfurled in his pounding heart. "I mean, how do you know she's actually pregnant?"

"You and Mom are on the same page. Even though Ellen showed her a positive result, my mother went out and bought her own tests and waited outside the bathroom while Ellen peed on the stick. She even nudged the door open and peeked inside to make sure she was using her own pee. Anyway, the result was positive."

Andrew wanted to scream, to run, to get in his car and drive somewhere, anywhere, without ever looking back. She might not have done it yet, but it was only a matter of time before Ellen announced who her baby's father was. She'd do it with relish, triumphantly. And Andrew's life would fall apart like a sandcastle against a relentless tide. His reputation would go first, and along with it, any hope of career advancement. His office was like that. And then, no matter the love between them, his family. Carrie could never get past this betrayal. And that meant, worst of all, his relationship with Jack would also be destroyed. The idea of losing his son was too painful to think about.

"They're coming here next weekend," Carrie said. "Just a quick two-day visit. It's the best way for my mother and I to confront her *together...* to convince her she's making a grave mistake."

Somehow Andrew was sitting on the couch again. He'd drifted there from the bar like a ghost, not even aware of the journey. A surge of dread coursed through him at the thought that his senses might be losing their ties to reality.

"I don't want her in this house," he said, voice trembling with suppressed fear and rage. "She caused enough problems the last time she was here."

And oh, God, would she love causing more problems on this visit. He could see her ugly face aglow with triumph, her eyes slinking between Carrie and their mother in this living room, her venomous voice making revelations no one would believe... at first. *"While you were at work, Andrew and I screwed around. That's right, Carrie, we fucked. You know what that means? It means this baby is* his."

"She's not only a madwoman," he continued, "she's also a bad influence on Jack. I don't want him hearing all of this shit."

"Andrew, please," Carrie said. "Jack won't be a part of the conversation. We'll go out for lunch or wait till he's at school. Don't worry about Jack. I wouldn't expose him to this."

"I. Don't. Want. Her. Here."

Carrie tilted her head. "I've seen you upset with her before and I know you don't like her. But this reaction is a little over the top, even for you. What's going on?"

"I don't like her. I never have and you know it. All she does is cause problems. Why can't they stay at a hotel? I'll pay for it."

She shook her head. "Because it's my mother and my sister and I can't ask them to stay at a hotel."

"You shouldn't have invited them to visit without talking to me first," Andrew said. "*I'll* tell them they have to stay at a hotel."

"No, you won't," Carrie shot back. "And another thing —"

The doorbell interrupted their argument. "That's the food we ordered," she said, turning for the door. "Where's Jack? He must be famished."

Andrew had almost forgotten they hadn't eaten dinner yet. They'd ordered Mexican maybe half an hour ago, when his world still made sense. The thought of chicken burritos and guacamole added a churn of nausea to the turmoil in his stomach.

He stood and joined Carrie at the door, where she grasped the plastic bags filled with takeout containers.

"They can't stay here, Carrie." He met her eyes. "If they're here, I won't be."

Shock and anger flashed in Carrie's gaze. "Fine, then leave. I really don't know why you're acting this way. My sick, unmarried, childish sister is pregnant, my mother and I are trying to handle the crisis, and all you're concerned about is them staying here? What's your issue, Andrew? Why are you so —"

A sound came from the staircase. On the top step, Jack leaned against the railing, staring at the two of them like a spectator watching a boxing match. But people who paid for match tickets usually didn't watch them with such confusion and sadness. Andrew even caught a shadow of fear there, an echo of the night terrors of the past.

"It's okay, Jack. Just a minor squabble," Carrie reassured him. "It's time to eat. I got you beef flautas with that spicy salsa you like."

The pressure that had been building in Andrew reached his head, a volatile mix of rage and fear threatening to burst through his skull. He patted his pants pocket, feeling the reassuring shape of his car keys.

"Can you see it now, Carrie?" He pointed at Jack descending the staircase. "Your sister hasn't even arrived and look at the problems she's already caused!" He shot a remorseful glance at Jack, regretting what he'd done with Ellen, why he'd done it, and what was going to break loose once Ellen and Michelle arrived. "I'm sorry, buddy, I just can't handle this." To Carrie, he said, "I need to leave before I lose my shit."

Without waiting for her response, he swung the door open and stepped out. He raced to his BMW and backed it down the driveway into the quiet suburban road. His heartbeat still echoed in his ears as he rounded the corner onto Elm Street, found a spot along the curb, and put the car into park.

Pressing the TALK button on his steering wheel, he breathed out a strained command, "Call Scott."

After two nerve-wracking rings, Scott's voice came through, hushed but *there*. "Hey."

"Hey," Andrew echoed. "I need you to meet me. Is there a way to slip out for a few?"

"We're just wrapping up dinner. Why? What's up?"

Andrew stared blankly at the colonial-style house across the street from where he was parked. "You're not going to believe it."

Hearing muffled noises on the other end, he pictured Scott moving away from the commotion of his household.

"Talk to me. What's going on?"

His voice dipped to a whisper, though he wasn't sure why. "Ellen's pregnant."

Silence.

"Scott?"

Scott's reply eventually came, barely more than a whisper. "No fucking way. You told me she said she couldn't get pregnant."

Andrew winced. "Yeah, she did. I was drunk, desperate to get it over with. She told me about having tube issues and not being able to have a baby, and I believed her. I have no excuse other than drunken stupidity. And now...here I am. Here we *both* are, stuck in this mess."

"Both?" asked Scott.

"Yeah, Scott. *Both*. Once Ellen opens her mouth about the baby and then about me, you think your name won't come up? I'm telling you, she's a nutjob on a rampage and doesn't care who she runs over along the way."

"Shit, Andrew." Andrew heard Scott's breath quicken. "Okay. I'll tell Jamie I have to go to the office for an hour or two. She knows we're working on a reorg for next quarter, so it shouldn't raise any red flags. I'll be at the Starbucks on Post Road in about twenty minutes. Try to keep calm. We'll think of something."

"We'd better." Andrew sighed heavily. "I'll see you in twenty."

After pressing the button on the steering wheel to end the call, he placed his elbow on the door's armrest and his chin on his fist. The colonial with its white clapboards stood against the twilight. The two brick chimneys punctuating the steep roof that rose so high they eclipsed some of the early stars. Down toward earth, the glowing windows hinted at a cozy life within.

Andrew knew the family who lived there, the Andersons, poster children for stability and contentment. But did they also have their secrets? Was their picture-perfect life a façade, hiding troubles as terrifying as his own? He'd overheard Carrie and Jamie sharing stories of neighbors with marital problems, abuse, a nervous breakdown popping up now and then. But the rumors never materialized, the people in this town too adept at keeping secrets, allowing its residents to live in blissful ignorance. That's because none of them had an Ellen in their lives. Someone who cared nothing about repercussions and was willing to destroy many lives with only a few words.

As he put the car in drive, Andrew clung to the hope that together, he and Scott could devise a strategy to deal with this ticking time bomb. He was prepared to do anything to prevent the catastrophe hurtling toward them.

Anything at all.

CHAPTER SEVENTEEN

The car was wrapped in silence, like a fly caught in silk on a spider's web, as Ellen drove them through the labyrinth of Philadelphia streets and onto I-95.

They'd made this trip to Darien many times before. It was a journey they were familiar with, a three-and-a-half-hour stretch that could feel like an eternity, boredom as painful as a pap smear. But this time around, Michelle would prefer boredom to the storm she sensed was about to break.

They hadn't spoken much since the day she made Ellen retake the pregnancy test and Michelle later threatened to throw her out. Michelle didn't expect the silence in the car to break, but unsaid words and emotions made the atmosphere crackle as if lightning was about to strike. She thought about the span of time ahead of them, the unending strips of highway, each passing mile marker counting the distance between mother and daughter. But Michelle didn't care. The revulsion she felt by Ellen's pregnancy, and the secrets behind it, lingered.

No matter how much she tried to get information from or reason with her daughter, she'd only get pushback and shouting. So rather than creating another battle of words, she tread cautiously which, for this trip, meant keeping the conversation to a minimum.

A few hours into the drive, Ellen began to punctuate the monotony with audible sighs and groans. Each sound grated on Michelle's nerves. Was it possible she despised her own daughter? Her own flesh and blood? She shook her head with an involuntary jerk to cut off the path her thoughts tried to take. It wasn't possible. It couldn't be.

Michelle's somber thoughts brightened when she peered out the windshield and realized her careful scheduling had paid off. Leaving home early to avoid the usual pockets of congested traffic had allowed them to make remarkable progress. They'd already reached Newportville, which meant they'd be crossing the Delaware River Bridge in a matter of minutes.

A sense of anticipation tingled in Michelle's veins as they reached the bridge. She sat up in her seat, her eyes shifting out the passenger-side window. The river's surface shimmered like pounded silver under the late morning sun — a natural beauty so contrary to the inside of the car in which she was trapped. And just as quickly as they approached it, they were leaving it behind, driving down the opposite slope of the bridge and back to a landscape of giant billboards and industrial buildings.

After another hour of moans and groans from the both of them, the monotony was broken when Michelle spotted signs for Enrico's, a restaurant in Edison, New Jersey, where they'd eaten lunch on previous trips to Connecticut.

"Why don't we stop there?" she asked, breaking their most recent bout of silence. "We love their pizza!"

Ellen rubbed her stomach. "Sounds good. I'm eating for two now."

Trying to ignore the pang of annoyance created by Ellen's comment, Michelle continued, "It's a beautiful day. We can sit outside at their picnic tables."

"And I can have that hot sausage."

Michelle couldn't help but roll her eyes at Ellen's mention of the topping she loved. It seemed so petty against the purpose of this journey — a mission for her and Carrie to persuade Ellen to reconsider her life-changing decision. What Ellen wanted on her pizza was at the bottom of Michelle's list of concerns, if it was anywhere on that list to begin with.

Ellen made a left onto Vista Drive, then the quick right onto Mill Road. The houses in the neighborhood around Enrico's were weather beaten, with paint fading and peeling, exposing the splintered wood beneath. On some homes, shutters hung loose on rusty hinges, attempting to shield broken windows that vacantly stared. Weeds had overrun most of the lawns and curled over the cracked paths, tracing overgrown routes up crumbled steps. Porches slanted under invisible weight, warped from many seasons of exposure.

"How can such a good restaurant be in the middle of such grossness?" Ellen asked.

"Seriously, Ellen? I know this isn't Rodeo Drive, but can't you just keep your negative opinions to yourself for a change? Do you have to say *everything* that's on your mind?"

"Whoa, calm down, Mommy Dearest. I'm just saying that I don't understand why they'd keep their business in such a shithole town. Why wouldn't they move to a nicer area?"

"People who live in glass houses shouldn't throw stones."

"What the hell does that mean?"

Michelle shook her head. "It doesn't matter." She pointed to an empty spot as Ellen turned into Enrico's parking lot. "Just pull in there. And please make sure only *half* the pizza has your sausages on it. I'd like cheese only on my slices, thank you."

Ellen shut off the car engine and turned to Michelle. "You're welcome," she said, holding out her palm.

Eyes closed to tamp down or at least hide her irritation, Michelle reached for the wallet inside her pocketbook, took out two twenty-dollar bills and held them out for her daughter to take.

"See you in a few!" Ellen shouted, hopping out the car door.

Michelle got out of the car and followed the narrow dirt path to the picnic tables where a dozen or so people devoured pizza, stromboli, calzones, and melting gelato. They sounded so cheerful, their chatter and laughter mingling with the delicious aromas in the air. Slipping onto a bench at a vacant table, Michelle slid her sunglasses up the bridge of her nose so they covered her eyes completely. Behind the dark lenses, she looked over the families gathered around her, each seemingly in their own bubble of happiness and love, nothing like the fractured bond she shared with Ellen.

Her eyes settled on two young girls playing hide and seek.

An ache formed in her chest as she was reminded of the days when Ellen and Carrie were just as carefree and content. A few months after she'd thrown Ben out, the two girls seemed happier, lighter, as though released from chains of oppression. They'd play games, just like the children around her now, laughing and cackling more inside a few days than she'd heard them do in years. Though not all their problems had disappeared. Ellen still struggled with her self-image and Carrie continued to refuse to acknowledge the effects of her father's actions. But Michelle let these issues lie. She'd first let her family enjoy the freedom she'd provided by fracturing her cheekbones with a rolling pin. Then she'd deal with the psychological problems later.

The "later" came when Ellen entered puberty. The depression and self-loathing she'd experienced before adolescence was nothing compared to what was happening now. She'd become a sullen and bitter teenager whose every word dripped with sarcasm and disdain. She was losing weight so quickly, Michelle brought her to a nutritionist who designed a special diet so Ellen would regain some of the weight she'd lost. It probably would have helped if Ellen followed the diet, but the girl was obstinate. She refused to listen to Michelle about anything, including her diet.

Utterly confounded, Michelle sought the help of a psychologist for guidance on how to handle her daughter. When Dr. Vance asked to meet with them both, Michelle closed her eyes and forced a laugh. "I already begged her to come with me. But no. She's too smart... she knows everything... she'll be 'fine' in just a few weeks. What am I supposed to do with that?"

"Don't give up. Keep asking!" was the only advice Dr. Vance could offer.

After eight months of therapy, Michelle and Dr. Vance determined Ellen's issues were potentially caused by a combination of factors. She could be suffering from the onset of major depression, the same ghost from Michelle's family history that made her mother take her own life with a bullet. Dr. Vance said that fifty percent of depression-related illness was hereditary. In a way, this gave Michelle hope. If it was depression, there were medications for that — medications her mother never took. Add to that the ribbing and harsh treatment Ben had inflicted on a daily basis, her envy toward a beautiful and popular older sister, and her fierce insecurities. Putting all this together had Michelle worried that Ellen could be heading down an even darker road, one mirroring the fate of her grandmother.

Though it pained her to be tough on her daughter, she had no other option than to force her to see a psychiatrist. Like it or not, it was the only way for both of them to live a semblance of a life.

"Do you want to smile again?" she asked Ellen.

No response.

"Do you want to have friends, go to parties, laugh, enjoy life...at all?"

Ellen rolled her eyes, sliding her legs away from her mother, to the other side of the bed on which Michelle sat.

"Well, I want you to have all those things. That's why you're going to see a psychiatrist I found. His name is Dr. Blout."

"I'm not going —"

Michelle interrupted. "You are going or I'm giving up."

Ellen let the magazine she was reading fall on her lap. "What do you mean 'giving up'?"

Michelle inhaled as she swallowed hard against the lump in her throat. *This is for your own good, Ellen.* "It means you're on your own. You make your own meals, clean your own clothes, get yourself to school, take care of yourself when you're sick. Like I said, on your own. I give up. We can live in the same house but that doesn't mean we have to talk to one another."

"What is this, blackmail? If I don't see a shrink you won't talk to me? I'm your daughter for God's sake!"

"And that's why I'm doing what I'm doing. You can call it blackmail if you'd like. I'd call it tough love. Deal with it or don't. It's up to you."

Michelle stormed out of the room. She forced herself not to turn around. This was too important. Her sessions with Dr. Vance helped confirm that her daughter's problems were not the normal teenage issues — they were deeper, darker, more severe than high school jealousies or peer pressure. She'd become agoraphobic, angry, mean, and hateful to anyone with whom she'd come into contact. Her energy level was close to zero, she had no motivation to do anything productive, including schoolwork, and her mood episodes would last for days to months at a time.

Michelle had no other choice. If she didn't put her foot down now, it could be too late before she had the chance to try it again.

That night, Ellen agreed to see Dr. Blout.

It took a year of experimenting with different medications and their complex side effects before Blout prescribed Fluoxetine. At first it was a godsend. For the next two years there were rays of hope, little bits of progress here and there. Despite the slight and periodic improvements, Michelle knew her daughter and could never shake the sense that Ellen still felt like a stranger in her own skin. The medication had stabilized her moods, but there was always something missing.

It was like Ellen simply *existed,* never really wanting to be independent, to find dreams to fulfill or a life of her own to live. She seemed content to live in Carrie's shadow and under Michelle's wing day after day. Decades passed before it became painfully clear that the meds couldn't help, nor could the therapy sessions with Dr. Blout. Ellen was stuck in Neutral and nothing or no one could shift her motivation into Drive.

Was it her own fault? Did she give in too often? Surrender to Ellen's demands too quickly? She had no answers and had pretty much given up — a support group her only outlet, guilt and anger the only emotions she could muster when it came to Ellen.

And now the weight on Michelle's shoulders grew heavier as Ellen's life veered in another direction, one that involved a child with no help from its father. She feared this situation might be the one to push her daughter over the edge — like it did her mother and *her* mother before that, a woman Michelle had only heard obscure tales about.

She stopped herself from going too far down this path: it would lead to her pitying Ellen, and that just played into her daughter's deficiencies. Michelle knew this was not the time to coddle her daughter. However bitter things became between them, she'd remain steadfast: she would not let Ellen live with her if she decided to keep the child. Michelle was too old, too exhausted. She'd be willing to let go of her daughter before sacrificing her own sanity, no matter how much it pained her. The only hope that remained, the only prospect of having any relationship with Ellen was that together, she and Carrie could dissuade her from going through with this disaster in waiting.

Eventually Ellen arrived and tossed the pizza box onto the table along with a handful of napkins, half of which fell on the ground. Without a hint of concern for the mess she'd just made, Ellen tore open the box and grabbed a slice with the spicy sausage. She folded it in half before taking an enormous, uninhibited bite. Oil dribbled down her chin, and the sight left Michelle feeling queasy.

"I'm going to go — pick up some paper plates," she muttered, getting to her feet. It was the first excuse she could think of to escape the scene.

When she returned, she placed a plate in front of Ellen.

"This is how human beings eat," she said in a hushed tone.

Ellen merely brushed off the remark, devouring another massive bite. "They eat like this, too. It's called pizza," she retorted, speaking around the threads of cheese stretching between her hand and mouth.

Michelle shook her head and took a few small bites of her own slice.

"Just as good as I remember it," she managed to say, finding a pleasant topic of conversation in the nostalgia that arose at the flavors. "One of the few restaurants in this world that's consistent."

Ellen nodded absentmindedly, threatening the stability of the sunglasses perched on the tip of her nose. She chewed with voracity, seeming oblivious to the other tables, the people who might judge her lack of table manners.

Michelle wasn't sure if she should continue trying to hold a conversation. *Screw it. I'm not going to just sit here and watch her chew like a cow.* "I feel like it's been so long since I've seen my family. I don't get to speak to Jack much, so I'm really looking forward to seeing him."

Ellen nodded again. "Yeah." She chewed harder. "He's the best part of *your* family."

Ugh. Michelle thought through her last comment. *Shit.*

"I meant *our* family." From Ellen's disregard of her words, she knew the damage had been done. "By the way, I was a little surprised you were so willing to come with me." She wasn't going to thank her, but she came close. "I know you were just there in March, but I think all of us being together is going to be really nice."

"And you're also hoping she'll talk me out of having a baby, right?" Ellen held Michelle's gaze while folding another slice of pizza.

A knot of unease tightened within Michelle, but she feigned surprise. "Why would you say that? Do you really think that's why I asked you to come with me?"

Ellen nodded. "Yeah, I do. You and Carrie might as well be joined at the lips... or ears. Or lips to ears. Whatever. I know the first thing you did when you found out I was pregnant was call Carrie. And now she's going to try to talk me out of having my baby. You both have it all figured out."

"Carrie and I didn't talk about her trying to talk you into or out of anything." Michelle hoped she'd managed to keep the strain of her lie from her voice, or that Ellen was too absorbed in the cheese she barely chewed to notice. "You can talk about it with her if you'd like. Or don't. Now I'm even more surprised you agreed to come. I mean, if you believed that Carrie was going to try to talk you out of having this baby, I'd think that would turn you off. I wanted you to come so I could spend some time with you, maybe try to reduce some of the friction we've had between us since... since... well, you know... since you told me about your condition."

Ellen's laughter pierced the surrounding conversations, so much more cutting than the giggles and snorts of families enjoying their lunches. She gulped down a swig of Pepsi, and Michelle could see a storm raging behind her sunglasses-darkened eyes. "The condition is called *pregnancy*. And I don't know about you, but the friction in the car has been pretty steady if you ask me."

"Why do you have to be such a smartass, Ellen?" Michelle retorted. "How do you expect to get along with *anyone* when you act this way? I mean, I'm your *mother* and your tone makes me want to slap you."

"You think you want to slap me now?" Ellen asked, folding her arms on the table. "Wait till you hear why I really wanted to come."

Michelle prayed the knot in her belly wouldn't tighten much more or she might vomit up her pizza. From the look on Ellen's face, she knew her prayer wasn't going to be answered.

"I want to see Andrew's face when we talk about it."

She reeled as if Ellen's words had been a slap, even as she struggled to grasp what they meant. "What on earth does Andrew have to do with this?"

"Promise you won't tell anyone?" Ellen lowered her voice to a near-whisper and seemed genuinely vulnerable when she asked.

"Tell anyone *what?*"

"Andrew's the father."

The world around Michelle seemed to blur, her heart pounding in her chest like a war drum. "Cut it out, Ellen. That's not even funny."

"That's because it's not a joke." She put her lips around the straw in her Pepsi can, sucked for a few moments, then swallowed and said calmly, almost casually, "He fucked me when I was there in March."

For all Michelle's body knew, an earthquake had shattered the ground beneath their picnic table. "What in God's name are you talking about?" she stammered.

"*I'm* going to keep it a secret. Forever. But if you don't believe me, you can ask Andrew yourself."

"Why on earth would I believe that insanity?" Michelle clasped her knees with trembling hands. "Andrew is a happily married man with a wonderful family. Why would he jeopardize that by sleeping with *you*?"

Ellen replied with continued nonchalance, "You can ask the happily married man's boyfriend."

"Ellen!" She struck the table with her fist, panic surging. How could she have found out that secret? Was there a way Michelle could *keep* it a secret? "Stop with these riddles and talking in circles. What the hell are you saying? Do you hate your sister *so* much that you'd make up a story like this?"

Giggling, she wiped the grease from her mouth with the back of her hand. "Poor, poor, Mom. You think you know everything about your precious daughter and her family, but things aren't as wonderful as they seem. Looks can be deceiving you know." She looked down and pointed her index finger toward her belly, a bubble of grease dripping from her chin onto her shirt. "Look at me, I'm pregnant and my stomach's so flat, no one would have any idea. Now *that's* not a 'story' as you call it, is it?"

Michelle's prayer for the knot in her stomach to not tighten any further went unanswered. It took everything she had to keep her pizza from making its way back up from where it came. "Ellen, I honestly don't understand why you insist on making up lies that —"

Ellen pushed her sunglasses up the bridge of her nose and continued, "Lies? I don't lie. You of all people should know that. Sins of omission, maybe. But not lies. When I was there in March, I found out Andrew has a boy toy on the side. I pretty much told him that if he didn't screw me, I'd tell Carrie. So he gave in, although he had to drink plenty first..." This time she used both hands to delineate her silhouette from face to waist. I mean, look at me. I'm not exactly a beauty queen." She picked a piece of melted cheese off a slice of pizza and dangled it above her open mouth. Slowly, she let it slide onto her tongue and then took her time chewing it, purposely making Michelle wait for the plot twist — an ending which no longer held an ounce of surprise. "I thought I couldn't get pregnant, so I told him he didn't have to use a condom. And voila, here we are."

"I literally feel sick to my stomach," Michelle choked out. Her insides boiled like a witch's cauldron full of poisonous herbs and animal parts. She kept her eyes off of what remained of their meal. "How could you do something like this? To your own sister, for God's sake?"

Ellen opened her mouth to respond, and she knew, she just *knew* it would be some more bullshit. Michelle raised her palm in her daughter's smiling face. "You know what? I don't even want to hear what you have to say. It would all be crap anyway. I'm talking, and you're going to listen. Do you realize you terrified a man into having sex with you? You blackmailed him, Ellen. *Blackmailed* him so you could...I don't even know or *want* to know why you did it. Because no matter what you say, it won't make sense. Nothing you do *ever* makes sense."

Undeterred, Ellen attempted to speak again, but Michelle talked over whatever she would have said. "Now, just so *you* know, Carrie knows all about Andrew's... well, his affair or whatever you want to call it. We've talked about it. She's learned to accept it, but decided not to talk about it with him. So your blackmail scheme was pointless. And now look what you've done."

Ellen's smile faded, her face draining of color. "Are you telling me she doesn't mind having a husband who screws around with men on the side?"

"We all have our reasons for doing and not doing things," Michelle said. "It's none of your business, or mine for that matter. She wants her family to stay together and there are things she's willing to put up with, as there might be things he puts up with where Carrie's concerned."

"That's absolutely ridiculous," Ellen said. "Everybody's so busy keeping secrets from each other so they can live a so-called happy life. Meanwhile, they're *miserable*. All my life, people have mocked me. In high school it was my weight. After that it was Maria telling me I was crazy and how she'd hear people talking about me: 'She has no friends,' 'What's wrong with her?', 'Why can't she act normal?'. You probably do the same thing at that support group you're running to all the time. Jesus, Mom. Is keeping secrets from your husband and lying to your wife 'normal?' Is bringing your kid up with that kind of thing going on 'normal?' Sit back and take a look around...who's really crazy in this family?"

"We're not even talking crazy right now," Michelle insisted. "We're talking evil, mean, depraved actions. Can you even comprehend what you've done? How sick it is to use extortion for sex? And you really think they'll never find out your baby is Andrew's? How's that supposed to work? I know *I* would never say anything, but you know you and your temper. One wrong word and you'll vomit the truth about his paternity in the blink of an eye. Plus there's the fact that you don't even have a boyfriend. Do you think Andrew is *that* ignorant that he won't know it's his?" Suddenly Michelle felt like someone had sucked all the air from her lungs. It was hard for her to breathe and she placed her hand on her chest. *Calm down. Breathe.* After a few seconds of self-talk, she felt better enough to speak. "I think we should turn around right now. I'll go visit them on my own."

"We're not turning around. I'll walk the rest of the way if I have to. I want to hear what Carrie has to say about my pregnancy. Maybe she *will* change my mind. Believe me. I have my doubts." A touch of vulnerability had entered Ellen's voice again. "Maybe she can push me over the fence to not having the baby. If I have you *and* her against me, I won't have anyone to help me and I'll *really* be screwed. And I promise. I swear I won't tell her it's Andrew's. I wouldn't do that... even to her."

With unsteady fingers, Michelle removed her sunglasses and brushed away the tears streaming down her cheeks. When it came to Ellen's words she didn't know what to believe and what to ignore. She lacked the strength to continue the fight. "Ellen, what did Carrie ever do to you that was so bad? Really, what did she do?"

"Jesus, Mom. You'll never understand." Ellen stood up and turned toward the path back to their car. "It's not what she did; it's what she *didn't* do."

CHAPTER EIGHTEEN

"Should you really be drinking, Ellen?" Carrie asked. Pretending to meticulously tuck potato slices around the meatloaf in the baking dish, her focus was really on Ellen's response.

Ellen sipped her vodka tonic before resting the tumbler on the kitchen island. Leaning on her stool, she laid her elbows on the cool polished quartz. Carrie raised her eyes from the potatoes she was arranging in the dish to meet her sister's gaze.

"Why? Because of the baby?" she shot back.

"Yes, because of the baby." Carrie slid the meatloaf into the oven and let the door slam shut. The sound echoed on the hard surfaces of the kitchen. "You poured your drink as soon as Mom went upstairs to lie down. It's like you know you shouldn't, but you did it anyway."

"And so what if I do?" Ellen took another swig of her drink. "I thought you were going to talk me out of having the baby. If that's going to happen, why should I stop drinking?"

Carrie took in a deep breath. To stand any chance of helping their mother persuade Ellen to change her mind, she had to keep her wits about her. "No one said anything about talking you out of it. Your defenses were up before I even opened my mouth."

"Well, let's see..." Ellen poured more vodka into her glass. Carrie wasn't sure whether her sister forgot the tonic this time around or had added it to her first drink as a pretense at diluting the alcohol. "We got here almost two hours ago. Your husband wasn't home to greet us, your son has been at some kind of rehearsal, and in all that time I haven't heard a 'congratulations' come out of your mouth. What am I supposed to think?"

"I don't know what you're supposed to think," Carrie replied, trying to keep her voice steady. "That's your business. I told you that Andrew's company has a big presentation tomorrow and they have to make sure it's perfect. Jack should be home within the hour. They can't stop rehearsal just because his aunt and grandmother are coming to town."

"Gee, Andrew always seems to have a presentation to prepare for."

Carrie took another deep breath and reached for her own wine. "That's part of his job. Since he's their top writer, he needs to be in on all the new client presentations."

"At least he says he does."

"What is that supposed to mean?"

"It means I don't trust people much. I never take anyone at their word. Do you check to make sure he's at the office?" she asked in a voice filled with insinuation.

"No, Ellen. I don't need to check up on my husband."

Ellen huffed.

"And that snide breath means?"

"I told you. I just don't trust people. They're always up to *something.*"

Ellen downed the rest of her drink and tried to sit up straight, pushing against the countertop. Once she was mostly upright, she set her glass down on the cool polished quartz. Its faint clink echoed, strangely stark against the backdrop of their heated exchange. Carrie watched her slowly slide off the stool, walk to the refrigerator and press her tumbler against the ice dispenser's lever. The soft grinding hum of the fridge's mechanisms filled the silence before ice fell into the glass.

Carrie couldn't understand how Ellen could keep knocking back glass after glass of vodka. If she kept drinking at this pace, it wouldn't be long — maybe another hour — before she'd be stumbling and tripping over her own feet. But what really worried Carrie was that if Ellen continued the pregnancy and continued drinking like this, the baby was going to suffer.

What was Ellen thinking? Why was she acting like this? Why couldn't she just think rationally, like anyone else would in her situation? Her sister had always lived in her own world, but it was getting scarier here along the borders where Ellen's universe and theirs met. Carrie pushed down her fear and concern before responding to her sister's last remark.

"Well, not trusting anyone may be *your* way of life, Ellen. But it's not *mine*. And honestly, I don't know why you think the way you do. I've spent hours thinking back to or childhood. The trauma you might have suffered as a child...as a kid...as a teenager, and I can't figure out why you despise people so much. Or I really should say, why you treat your family the way you do. I know our father wasn't a dream dad and he didn't treat us the way we would've liked to be treated, but he never physically abused us." Carrie paused. "I should say, I never *let* him abuse me. If anyone should have trauma from that piece of shit, it's *me*."

"Oh. Is mental abuse not enough?" Ellen asked, sitting back down on the stool.

"I don't think he mentally abused us. He just acted out in ways —"

"He never mentally abused *you*. No one ever mentally abused you. I got the brunt of it."

"I don't remember it that way. We'll never see things the same way, whether back then or right now, at this moment." She watched her sister take another drink and blot away the alcohol dampening her lips, always thin and now narrowed to a razor. "We used to be close and now it's become impossible for us to see eye to eye on anything. I just don't get it."

Ellen sighed. "And you never will. Now why don't you just get to it and tell me why I shouldn't have this baby?"

Carrie tried to assemble her scattered thoughts. "I'm not going to tell you whether or not you should have this baby, Ellen. It's not my place. I just have two questions." She held her words, giving Ellen the time to finish swirling the vodka in her mouth. After the swallow, she asked, "Why won't you tell Mom, or me, who the father is? Does the man know, and shouldn't he be involved in this whole thing?"

"Why is knowing who the father is so important?"

"Really?" Carrie decided to speak honestly to avoid having the conversation go around in circles. "You rarely leave the house, you don't have many, if any, friends. Mom says you'll go shopping or see a movie sometimes. How the hell did you meet someone and get pregnant? Did it happen at the house? Did you meet him on a hookup app? Did you —"

"Like I told Mom, it's none of anyone's business. I know you have the perfect marriage with the perfect husband and perfect sex life." Ellen smirked. The expression and her words sent a chill up the back of Carrie's neck. "But I'm not you. I have to jump through hoops to get a man to fuck me. And I don't want this guy involved. If I do end up having this kid, I'll do it on my own."

"On your own? That's rich, Ellen. Do you have any idea what's involved in bringing up a child? The physical and emotional stress? The money you'll need for food, medical bills, clothing, schooling, and that's just the start. Right now you have no money, and you can't expect me or Mom to pay these bills. How do you expect to take care of your child's needs for the next eighteen years?"

Ellen offered no response, the silence broken only by the sound of her sipping her drink.

"You have no answer. And that's the problem. It's hard enough to bring up a child when you have a husband to help and money in the bank. The crying at night, the diapers, the cleaning, the breastfeeding. When they start to grow up, you have the school, teachers, and after-school activities. Then when they get older, there's the moodiness, the sarcasm, the texting which is so much more important than the words you're saying to them, the —"

Carrie abruptly stopped talking when she noticed Jack in the doorway. Ellen followed her gaze, swiveling around to see him. Her eyes flicked back to Carrie, and another smirk tugged at the corners of her mouth, a soft snicker escaping her lips.

"How much did you hear?" Carrie asked.

"Enough." Jack turned to her sister. "Hi, Aunt Ellen," he said with a hint of upset, then turned around and headed toward the stairs.

"Hey, Jack," Ellen said after him.

"Jack," Carrie shouted. "I hope you know I wasn't talking about you."

There was no reply, just the rhythm of his footsteps retreating up the staircase.

"Shit. Now I'm going to have to deal with that." She looked at Ellen. "See? It's all part of bringing up a kid. And if it's a girl, you're in the for ride of your life," she added, turning around to check the meatloaf in the oven.

"How could you say that? We're both girls!" Ellen asked.

"That's exactly my point."

Jack's mom carefully placed the meatloaf on a trivet in the center of the table. To his left sat Aunt Ellen, glass in hand, staring at her empty plate. His grandmother was on his right, ogling the meal as if it were a work of art.

As Carrie sliced into the meatloaf, the noise of the knife hitting the bottom of the dish carved through the silence. She divided it into portions and transferred each generous, steaming slice onto the dishes. After filling everyone else's plates, she sat down and placed a napkin on her lap. Jack looked between his mother and grandmother, their faces both masked with smiles that hid anger... or disgust... or... He really didn't know what they were thinking and trying to guess would only make him more anxious. But the one thing he did know for sure was that whatever was bothering them had to do with Aunt Ellen's drinking. Their eyes kept tracing the path of her vodka glass from the table to her lips. Every lift of the tumbler, each sound of a sip made their expressions tighten as if they'd been insulted.

He knew his mom had worked hard on this meal, but he was rapidly losing his appetite.

Instead, his stomach was full of nervous energy, an unpleasant hot buzz. Except for the movement of forks and knives and glasses, the room was still. But he felt the tension humming in it, rising and falling in a symphony conducted by his aunt lifting alcohol to her mouth.

"So, you're having a baby?" he asked Ellen. His courage to speak through the tension surprised even him.

She nodded and slurred, "Yes, s-sir. Looks like you're gonna ha-have a cousin."

"Cool," Jack said, though his heart pounded in his chest. He glanced at his mother and grandmother. Frustration had etched deeper into their faces, and his mom caught his eyes and shook her head. That was typically her signal to let go of an uncomfortable or dangerous topic.

He placed a potato on his tongue, hoping the flavors of cilantro and garlic would liven up his taste buds. It helped a little, but not enough to bring up the hunger he usually had this time of the day. Aunt Ellen was drinking without eating. She just stared at the glass in her hand or at the plate on the table, and hadn't been able to say more than two words without slurring. His mother and grandmother seemed so annoyed and angry they were playing with their food instead of eating it. He wanted to jump up and leave, get away from them all, but knew he'd get in trouble if he even tried.

"How's school?" his grandmother asked.

Oh, great, the "how's school?" question — a clear sign there was nothing else to talk about and he'd just become the main topic of conversation. Jack just managed to avoid making everything worse by rolling his eyes.

"Grammy asked you a question," Carrie said.

"Fine," he replied before placing a piece of meatloaf in his mouth to buy time. Once he'd chewed and swallowed, he asked, "When's Dad coming home?"

"He'll be home later tonight. He has this major —" Carrie began.

"Yeah, yeah. Huge presentation tomorrow, right?" God, he was sick of this shitshow. "Meanwhile, you almost wouldn't let me go to my rehearsal because Grammy and Aunt Ellen decided to —"

"Watch it, young man! That's no way to speak at the dinner table, especially in front of your grandmother and aunt. It's downright disrespectful!"

He shot an apologetic glance at Michelle. "Sorry."

Ellen was sipping more vodka as she tried, unsuccessfully, to hide her laughter. *Man, there is something* so *wrong with her.* He let his fork drop onto his plate with a clatter.

"Sorry," he repeated, this time addressing his mom. He wished Dad was there to add some common sense and humor to offset what was going on at this table.

Michelle cleared her throat and said brightly, "I hear you're the best Tony to have ever appeared on a stage."

"I wouldn't say the best," he mumbled, blushing. But it was better than whatever the hell had been happening before.

"Well, according to your parents, Aunt Ellen, and the glowing school newspaper review your mother sent me, it appears you *are* the best."

Jack skewered a potato slice with his knife as a smile crept onto his face. "Okay, well, maybe I am."

"*West Side Story* is one of my favorite movies of all time. Did you know it's based on Shakespeare's *Romeo and Juliet?*"

After gulping down his potato, Jack took a hearty swig of water. "Yes, I did. There are actually lines in the play that come from *Romeo and Juliet*."

Michelle dabbed her lips with a napkin and propped her chin on her hands. "Really? Could you share one?"

"There's a scene where Maria says to Tony, 'I forgot why I called you,' and I...I mean Tony...says, 'I'll wait till you remember.' It's almost the same as in Romeo and Juliet, when Juliet says, 'I have forgot why I did call thee back,' and Romeo says, 'Let me stand here till thou remember it.'"

"Wow," Michelle said. "You really *have* done your research."

Carrie chimed in, "Which is why he's the best Tony this town has ever seen."

Jack's pride painted the smile on his face broader. "And then there's the end, when Tony and Chino lift and close the gate where the rumble is going to happen. Their fates are sealed. Chino kills Tony and will spend his life in jail, his hope for a better future...poof...gone in seconds. It's the same as when Romeo and Paris are at Juliet's tomb and Romeo kills Paris. He realizes he has nothing to live for, so he takes poison and dies as he's kissing Juliet."

"Wow, there really *are* a lot of parallels. In these plays *and* how they might relate to real life." Carrie said. "It's so sad to see a young man die for love.

"Ob-bviously," Ellen added. She leaned over her still-full plate. "D-do you think your mom and dad are l-like Romeo and Juliet?"

"Ellen!" Michelle said.

"What? I'm ju-just asking if he thinks his pa-rents are in love like Ro-meo and Juliet. Li-like Tony and Maria. Wha-t's wrong with that?"

Michelle sighed, shaking her head. "If I need to tell you what's wrong with that, there's no use trying to explain it to you. Now why don't you eat something to absorb some of that alcohol you shouldn't be drinking?"

Silence cloaked the room again.

Jack broke it by saying, "Yes, I do."

"Do what?" Ellen asked, squinting at him.

"I think my mom and dad are just like Romeo and Juliet," Jack said.

Eyes gleaming, his mom reached out to cover his hand with hers.

"Oh?" asked Ellen. "So you're...you're saying your father would drink poison if he thought your mom left...died somehow?"

"I think they're totally in love. That's all. And any stuff that might get in the way doesn't matter. They would do whatever it takes to be together, in life...or in death."

CHAPTER NINETEEN

"Where's my journal?"

The desperation ringing in Ellen's voice sent shivers down Michelle's spine. Heart racing, she watched her daughter tear through her travel bag, throwing its contents all over the guest room bed. Shorts, T-shirts, and ankle socks covered the floor and chair beside the window. The dim light from the bedside lamp cast eerie shadows across chaos.

Michelle tried to maintain a sense of calm by carefully unpacking her own suitcase. Her fingers trembled as she placed her clothes in the dresser drawers while behind her, Ellen's agitated search continued. She swallowed hard, her mother's instinct insisting she find a way to comfort her daughter, but she felt lost and defeated. From the moment she was born, there was never a way to comfort Ellen.

"Why would you have brought it?" she asked. "I thought you didn't write in it. You said Dr. Blout was full of shit and writing your thoughts down wouldn't help you." So why was finding it suddenly so urgent?

Ellen continued digging through her bag, checking and rechecking the side pockets, even turning it upside down to make sure it was empty. "Shit! I wr-wrote in it yesterday before we left. It was the fir-irst time I wrote in it. And now...now it's...it's gone."

Michelle couldn't help but wonder if Ellen was telling the truth, or if she had even brought the journal. "Are you sure you packed it?" she asked and immediately wanted to take back her question.

Ellen snorted with annoyance. "Yeah, I-I'm sure. I wouldn't be lo-looking for it if I wasn't sure."

As Michelle hung her shirts in the closet, she was too worried to hold herself back from saying, "Maybe if you drank a little less, you'd have a better idea of where you might have left it."

"You know, Mom, you-you can blow it out your —"

Her drunken slur cut off at the sound of the front door opening downstairs. "Oh, what do you...you know. Mr. Andrew decided to come h-home tonight," she said, tossing her satchel on the chair. "I wonder if he finished his present-ation...or whatever he was *really* doing."

"Stop it, Ellen." She sighed. "I knew we should have turned around when we were at Enrico's. Coming here with you was a mistake. You're just a troublemaker, pure and simple."

"Am not," Ellen retorted and fell back on the bed, her face twisted with anger and hurt.

Michelle sighed and placed her suitcase inside the closet. "Just wash up and go to bed," she suggested. "We're here for a nice visit. Can you please try not to act mean or say things that only make people angry at you? Just for once?"

She could see the turbulent sea in her daughter's eyes, and knew that pushing her further would only lead to disaster. "I'm sorry. Let's just keep calm and get ready for bed. No need to stir things up tonight."

"*I'm* stirring things up? Me? You missed Ca-arrie standing in the middle of the kitchen, telling me how bringing up a kid is like-like torture. And she's saying it right in front, right in front of her own son."

"What are you talking about? When did that happen?"

Ellen glanced at her sidelong, and Michelle couldn't help but notice the stark contrast of the dim lamplight and deep shadows that played across her features. Exhaustion and the weight of her emotions were carved across her features, and for a moment, Michelle felt a surge of compassion for the struggles Ellen had faced and was confronting right now. At the same time, she couldn't help but burn with frustration because so many of those struggles had been caused or exacerbated by Ellen herself.

"She was starting her 'don't have a baby' spee-ech. Jack heard every word." Ellen *tsked*. "Poor kid. Poor Jack. Wait until he finds...finds...out that Carrie's Romeo is my baby's daddy."

"Ellen!" Michelle snapped, working to keep her voice down. "You said you wouldn't say anything. How does that mind of yours work? One second you say no one will ever know the truth, and the next, you're getting ready to share it with the world. What the hell is wrong with you? Have you no compassion?"

"None."

"Jesus, Ellen. First you blackmail Andrew by telling him you'll reveal his affair with a man and then you..."

Before Ellen could respond, something creaked faintly outside the room. Both mother and daughter turned their heads toward the door. Had someone heard them?

Michelle didn't see or hear anything more, but finally curiosity pushed her to step into the hallway and look around.

There was nothing in either direction.

She stepped quietly toward Carrie and Andrew's room at the other end of the long hallway. Their voices drifted to her, and her stomach turned over as she realized they were arguing.

"I don't want to see her," Andrew was saying. "I can't stand the sight of her. It makes me ill."

Michelle's heart ached at the words and their implications. Was Andrew being so cruel because he knew the truth about the baby?

"But my mother's here, too!" Carrie pleaded. "Can't you just stick around tomorrow morning for a few minutes? At least to say hello to Mom?"

Their room fell into silence, and Michelle saw Andrew storm out of the bedroom and into the small reading nook they'd built to the side of it. As he stared out the windows, he swayed from foot to foot, his agitation barely contained. Michelle hesitated, her heart torn between wanting to comfort him but fearful of getting too close in case he brought up things she'd have to lie about.

Overwhelmed, she turned away and walked back down the shadowy hall. As she passed, she peeked into Jack's room, finding it dark and empty. She sighed and returned to the guest room, closing the door behind her, the soft click of the latch sealing her and Ellen within.

Ellen, still sitting on the mattress, tilted her head —

threatening her balance — and asked, "Whattayagot? Who's out there?"

Michelle's exhaustion and emotions hit her hard and she fell onto the bed before her legs gave in. "This was a bad idea," she confessed, her voice trembling. "I think we should go home tomorrow."

Ellen stood up and stepped toward her, reaching out for the wall as she teetered. "What? Wh-why? We drove all the way here, and now we're just gonna...gonna turn around and go home?"

"Yes, exactly." Michelle said. The tremor in the back of her neck told her she'd reached her limit. The burden of her daughter's secret had become too heavy. She could barely lift her head from the mattress. And she didn't want to in case Andrew and Carrie started fighting again. The only thought that brought her solace was that her grandson wasn't in his room to witness the chaos Ellen had created.

"Why? Why would —"

"Ellen, your sister and her husband are fighting at the other end of the house. And guess what the topic is?" She didn't give her time to guess. "You. That's who they're fighting about. And that's before you tell them something that will destroy their lives forever. I swear, Ellen, you have the conscience of a gnat. If I wasn't so tired, I'd get in the car and drive us home this second."

Ellen's skeletal features grew even more hollow with anger. "Well, isn't that nice to hear fr-from my own mother? Talk about no compassion. Jesus, I need a drink."

"No, you don't!" Michelle yelled as Ellen headed toward the door.

"I know what I do and d-don't need. What I need...what I need is something to help me forget what just came out of your mouth. Maybe I'll fi-find my journal down there too. Thanks to you, I now have a shitload to write."

Michelle watched her daughter unlatch the door and step into the hallway, then vanish down it, her silhouette fading into the shadows lurking inside the vastness of the house. *Well, that could have gone better. How though? What have I done? What am I doing?* She stood up, stumbled to the chair by the window and dropped onto it, which meant she ended up sitting on Ellen's empty satchel, but she couldn't summon the energy to even pull it out from under her. Michelle did the only thing her body would let her do at that very moment — hang her head and cry.

Ellen closed the door behind her louder than she meant to. Her hand lingered on the knob for support as she turned her head to look down the sprawling, gloomy hallway. She blinked, trying to encourage her eyes to adapt. She slid her hand along the wall to her left, then grabbed the railing on the right of the catwalk as soon as she felt a slight chill, the cooler air rising from downstairs, signaling she'd reached the stairs.

At first the railing felt unsteady under her hold. She saw a flash of the night when she fell down the stairs in March. Back then she was in the center of the staircase holding onto nothing, grasping for the railing but only swiping space and air on both sides. Tonight she'd take extra precautions. Before taking another step, she tried shaking the banister to make sure it could hold her, serve as her lifeline in case she tripped.

When she felt confident enough that the railing wouldn't let her fall, she continued walking. One step, then another into the shadows beneath her. Soon, she'd have more vodka in her system and finally be able to speak her truth. Once her colorless friend from the glass bottle warmed her veins, untangled her vocal cords, loosened up the knot in her throat, she'd say the words she couldn't before. The blockade her mother tried building would be demolished. No more fucking hiding... for any of them.

Trying to descend another step, she looked across the living room, dusted in dim gold from the porch light streaming through the curtains. Beyond it, she saw her destination, the dark kitchen where the bottle loyally awaited her arrival. It just seemed so far away. The entire first floor of her sister's house was at the bottom of a fathomless abyss.

What was it, twenty steps? Might as well have been two hundred.

It didn't matter because vodka made this more than a worthwhile descent. But the most important thing right now was not to make the same mistake as last time. Falling down these stairs again would just prove everyone else was right — that she was a mess. They didn't always say it out loud; they didn't have to. She saw it in the way her mother rolled her eyes while watching her enjoy her drinks or how her sister got quiet when she came downstairs after a night of overdoing it a bit. After dislocating her shoulder during her last visit, she promised Carrie that she wouldn't allow herself to get that drunk again. Right now, she had a chance to prove herself. All she had to do was successfully make her way down to the bottom step. Easy.

Something creaked. She looked back in the direction she'd come from, but there was no one there. Just closed doors all along the hall. The sound must've just been the house settling, making itself a little more comfortable in its peaceful slumber. Ellen turned back to the staircase. She had to make that her only focus. Get down all the steps and pour a drink. Then she'd wake everyone up if she had to and say what needed to be said. It probably wouldn't be elegant — no, it definitely wouldn't be elegant. But it didn't have to be. It just had to be the truth.

She tightened her grip on the banister and inhaled, running the fingers of her other hand through the bird's nest of thin hair atop her head. She lifted her right foot, then allowed its weight to bring it down to rest gently on the first step. So far, so good. Her knees felt weak, but her grip on the railing helped to keep her balance. It prevented her from tumbling twenty steps down to the shadowy floor below.

With intense concentration, she lifted her other foot and placed it on the second step. A gasp escaped her lips as she rocked forward, surprised by the sneaky tug of gravity. In her teetering, her toes slipped over the edge of the step, but her fingers still grasped the solid wood beside her. She pulled herself back to being vertical, or as vertical as she could manage, and wobbled in place for a few seconds. Her heart raced, and her breath was heavy. She felt as if she'd scaled an icy cliff and just avoided falling onto sharp rocks thousands of feet below.

She was going to be fine. This was nothing compared to the night she wandered home in the early morning hours during a snowstorm with a blood alcohol level twice what it was now. This was as easy as falling off a log, and she was sure she'd make it to the first floor of this house. Well, *almost* sure.

Ellen raised her left foot and was just about to rest it on the next step when she felt a squeeze around her right wrist — the one above the hand on the railing she used to steady herself. Someone was standing behind her.

Someone yanked her hand off the banister so quickly, Ellen swayed, her right hand grasping for anything to keep her from falling. She had almost regained her balance when the shove came at her back.

The steps before her raced up with incomprehensible speed. The wrought iron balusters and the faint golden light that shone between them joined in a blur.

A scream came out of Ellen's mouth with all the breath that hadn't been knocked out of her. *Help,* she meant to shout, but she didn't hear anything that sounded like a word. This couldn't actually be happening, could it? Was this all part of her vodka-induced stupor? Maybe the room was just still spinning, and she only felt like she was falling. Yeah, that had to be it.

But that didn't explain the hand that had grabbed her or the forceful shove from behind.

Or the pain as her body slammed against stairs, only to keep falling.

As much as vodka could be a messy bitch, it didn't push her. It didn't take hold of her arm. It could make her miss a step and give gravity a chance to take control. But what was happening now wasn't because of a slip or a fall.

Some*one* made her fall, not the bottle downstairs.

As Ellen tumbled like wet towels in a clothes dryer, she caught sight of a leg. But before she could figure out whose it was, her skull smashed down hard on one of the treads. First she heard a crack before the pain pierced her neck. Then she heard another. This one, however, wasn't followed by any more pain.

In fact, the agony had stopped somehow, as if she'd left it behind on the stairs above. Been cut off from it. As if the part of her that felt pain — or anything else — had snapped away.

Once she reached the bottom of the staircase, there was nothing left of Ellen but a pair of eyes staring blankly at the shadows that crept like ghosts across the ceiling above the landing.

Footsteps. If she could feel fear, maybe she'd have felt it then, or maybe hope. *Are they going to help?*

A scream. It turned into words. She recognized Jack's voice. What was he saying? In an attempt to narrow her focus so she could understand his words, she tried to close her eyes, but they wouldn't shut. She tried with them open.

"Why aren't you doing anything?" he was shouting. "Get down here! Call 9-1-1!"

Somewhat more solid ghosts eclipsed the ghosts on the ceiling. But Ellen's vision was growing murkier; a light was turned on and lanced her eyes, making everything blur even more.

Amid the smearing shapes of people around her, the muddle of voices, her thoughts went to her journal. *I was right.* A single clear point of truth within her mind's chaos. *I am so alone.*

With those words, she let her mind follow her body into the smear of numb fog and darkness.

EPILOGUE

Jack sat in his trailer, the calm eye in the hurricane of the movie set.

He'd made sure the decorator took his penchant for elegant minimalism into consideration when designing the space. Eliminating unnecessary visual distractions that could force his mind to wander or trigger anxiety allowed him to concentrate more on his craft. The only photograph in the trailer, sitting on the glass side table beside his favorite chair, was a black-and-white image of his mother taken five months before her passing. He picked it up, handling it carefully by the frame, and stared at her beautiful face, vibrant with life and hope for an exciting future — both cut short by the aggressive cancer. It had been so unfair. But then, so was plenty of what happened in this world. Jack understood.

Holding back tears, he placed the photo back on top of the table. His heart hurt, thinking how much Carrie would've enjoyed sitting next to him, relishing his company and his success. At thirty years old, he'd become one of the most sought-after actors in the industry, and the only thing stopping him from fully enjoying his achievements was her absence.

Since Jack hadn't spoken to his father in over five years — not even when his mom was in hospice, or when he planned her funeral — he didn't know where Andrew was living. Nor did he care. Once that man's secrets had all come to light, Jack could barely stand to look at him, let alone talk to him. *It's better this way*, he would tell himself. *It's better this way.* The fact of the matter was, he wasn't sure if it was better and didn't have the nerve to find out.

He scribbled that last thought down in the light brown leather journal in his lap, then wrapped the suede golden cord around the book to close it.

A twinge of hunger made him to glance over at the kitchenette, where a bowl filled with fruit and protein bars sat on the counter. Blech. He was so sick of eating healthy for the part he played in this movie. "Stay lean and mean!" the director Franz would repeat every day after sending the nutritionist in for his daily diet inspection. He couldn't wait for filming to be over tomorrow so he could get back eating his favorite carbs... and, of course, ice cream. Refusing to eat another protein bar, he leaned back in the velvet chair and set his legs on the ottoman.

The trailer was the epicenter of Jack's transformative process, a sanctuary where the problems of the outside world ceased to exist and the character he played took center stage. From the wardrobe where bright costumes contrasted with the soothing neutral palette of his furniture, to the chrome fixtures of the tiny bathroom and cleverly petitioned sleeping area, it was all exactly the way he'd imagined his trailer since his first day at Julliard. It was a vision he'd use to help embody his dream of a successful career... of fame... of respect. It was the image he'd share with his mother, promising her, that nothing would get in the way of living the life he yearned for since the days he played Tony in *West Side Story*. And nothing did.

When three taps sounded on the trailer door, Jack slid the journal between the cushion and the arm of his chair. Leaning toward the side table, he grabbed the script off the square marble top.

"Come in!" He turned toward the door.

It opened and his agent peeked her head in. "Busy?"

"For you? Never too busy. Come on in."

Donna settled gracefully into the velvet armchair mirroring his across the coffee table. From the first time they'd met, he found comfort in her presence, a sense of belonging, though also a puzzling nostalgia. Donna was his age, yet from the moment he met her, there was an undeniable likeness to his mother. Was it her golden-blonde hair? Her hazel eyes, even when tired, mesmerizing, as if they held a thousand untold tales? Or was it her lips, almost always in a soft smile, the most unsettling similarity, with their echo of his mother's resilient joy? Perhaps it was the combination of them all, evoking a sense of warmth within him, a flickering ember of his childhood. It was as though she'd come into his life to look after him, never filling the void left by his mother, but at least offering her presence, her guidance and support, in its place.

"How are you doing?" she asked, a mundane question from anyone else, but filled with real compassion from Donna.

He let the script fall onto his lap. "I'm doing fine. What about *you*?"

"Grinding away to keep your star shining." She leaned back

into the velvet embrace of the armchair. "The grapevine says you'll be wrapping up this week."

"The grapevine is correct." Jack nodded. "One more day in front of the camera, and it'll be a wrap. It stretched us thin, took a little longer, but the tweaks and fine tuning, they'll definitely make this a better movie."

"That's great to hear. The buzz for this movie is absolutely crazy." Her excitement filled the trailer, a honeybee hum. "The hype is viral on every platform, headlines on every news outlet."

Pinching the bridge of his nose, Jack chuckled. "Yeah, I figured it would be. Three interviews a day tucked between shoots...but you probably knew that, since you're the one who scheduled them."

"Guilty as charged!" She rose and sauntered to the mini-fridge, where she gestured toward its door. "May I?"

"You don't even have to ask. This trailer is as much yours as it is mine."

She took a bottle, opened it and swallowed a generous gulp. "I'm sure I've said this, but it bears repeating: ever since the release of *Silent Jury* and then *Plenty of Time,* you are in high — and I mean *high* — demand. Which is why I'm here this afternoon."

Jack idly flicked the corners of the script pages, but the snapping sound they made was so abrupt it startled him. Trying to conceal his jolt, he sat forward. "I'm listening."

"Paramount wants you as the lead in a thriller they have planned for release in about eighteen months." She took another sip of water as a dramatic pause, allowing him a moment to digest the news.

"Interesting..." He kept his tone casual even as his pulse

quickened. "Paramount, you say? You know I'm *very* selective with the roles I accept." Jack grinned. "What's it about?"

"The plot has many layers, with several storylines happening at the same time. But I'll try to simplify things for both our sakes. You'll portray a man married to a wealthy woman, a man who commits adultery. The only one who knows about your infidelity is your sister. Before she gets to take the final step of revealing the secret to your wife, who is her best friend, you stop her in the most drastic way: murder. It's the only way to stop her from ruining your life and your future. The movie then follows you for the next decade...an existence burdened with guilt and its torment but most importantly, you having to cover up the crime you committed. That's where the plot's twists and thrills come in. It shows all the things you have to do, and the people who suffer, as you work to conceal the murder of your own sibling who wanted nothing more than to tell the truth."

Jack's hand slipped into the gap between the cushion and armrest as Donna's voice faded in his ears. His fingers found the familiar texture of the journal's leather cover, and it carried him fifteen years into the past.

His mom's words to Aunt Ellen rang in his head. "Then when they get older, there's the moodiness, the sarcasm. And then there's the texting. Typing non-stop as you try to talk to them."

She couldn't be talking about him. He wasn't *that* much trouble. Was he? No. She was just trying to convince Aunt Ellen not to have a kid. Yeah, that was it. He'd overheard his mother talking about it with Grammy on the phone a few days ago. This was her way of making it sound as though having a kid was worse than it really was. *Just like mom*, he thought, justifying her statements, *always exaggerating to get a point across*.

He climbed the stairs, his backpack hanging heavily from one shoulder. Grammy was just emerging from the guest room, rubbing her eyes, clearly still groggy from a nap. But the moment she saw him, her eyes brightened and she spread her arms, inviting him in for a hug. He stepped into it, and she kissed his cheeks twice. In between the kisses she paused to look at his face with a sunny smile. Then she pulled him into another hug, this one so tight he had to gasp for breath.

"My goodness, how you've grown!" She stepped back and kept her hands on his arms so he wouldn't move as her eyes drank him in — like a work of art brought to life. "You're beautiful...I mean, handsome. Absolutely gorgeous."

He smiled and placed a gentle kiss on his grandmother's cheek.

As he started to pull back, she caught his chin in her hand. "Why the sourpuss face?" she asked gently. "I thought you'd be excited to see your Grammy!"

"I am," he said, the words his mother spoke to Aunt Ellen still sticking within crevasses inside his head. "It's just been a long day."

She playfully messed up his hair and kissed his cheeks for the third time. "I hear you, hon. Go put your stuff away and come downstairs. I'd love to catch up a little before dinner."

"Be there in a sec," he said, heading for the refuge of his bedroom.

After throwing his backpack on the bed, Jack walked stiffly back to the door. Glancing out of it, he saw Grammy descending the stairs. Was she going to join forces with Mom against Ellen and throw out more reasons not to have a kid? And why didn't they want her to have a baby, anyway? Sure, she was a mess and drank a lot, but maybe having a kid would help her get her life together. *Something* had to do it. Why wouldn't they even —

His questioning triggered the sudden rush of a vivid memory — his mother sneaking a peek at Aunt Ellen's journal. Maybe she'd read something that made her think it was a really bad idea for Aunt Ellen to have a baby. What did it say? What had his aunt written that might make his mother *and* grandmother so against her having a kid? He looked side to side and then down the stairs, listening carefully until he heard all three voices.

They were all downstairs and now, with the coast clear, he turned and headed toward the guest room. Although he was sure everyone was in the kitchen, he continued to twist his head around and glance behind him, worried someone might come looking for him or has possibly forgotten something upstairs. After one last look, he slipped into the guest room, scanning it for Aunt Ellen's travel bag. He found it in the center of the bed, looking like a homeless person's weathered satchel or like something abandoned on the roadside that had been cooked by the sun and exhaust fumes.

Jack stepped toward it, careful not to let his footsteps make a sound. As he reached the bed, he darted another glance at the door to make sure nobody was in the hallway. He leaned over the bed, pulled the bag toward him and unlatched its straps. The inside was divided into compartments; one of them bulged with something that seemed the right shape and size. He carefully unsnapped it, and there was the journal, tied with its cord. Once Jack unwrapped it, the journal fell open. He flipped through the pages and found four of them filled with scribbling. The rest were blank.

He went back to the front and began reading. The words he read sent a sweaty chill up the back of his neck.

*"It's all about family. Family staying together is number one priority."
That's all my sister ever says. But she's talking about* her *family. Her
little, picture perfect family. A family* I'm *not a part of.*

She was so angry. It was like she hated her own family. His
stomach cramped and the tension in his neck was making his
head ache. The words made him uncomfortable, oddly irritable
actually, and he wanted to stop reading. But he found himself
unable to put the book down.

*Andrew hates me most of all. I get it. He actually always hated me.
And now — holy crap, I can't even write about what's going on 'cause my
hands would shake too much. If anyone wants me off this planet, it's him.
He's probably the only one who would do it with his bare hands, too, after
what I did. But if he killed me, Jack would grow up with a father in
prison. Would he do that to his only child?*

Jack's heart skipped a beat and he almost dropped the
journal when his mother's voice called from downstairs: "You
coming down, Jack?"

His hands trembled as he slammed the book shut and rushed
from the guest room into his own bedroom. There he tucked the
journal into his backpack, wiped his eyes with his palms and
shook his head. *Holy shit.*

"Coming!" he yelled back.

Later that night, as he was reaching in his backpack for Aunt
Ellen's journal, he heard her arguing with Grammy down the
hall. Although he could hardly wait to continue reading what
she'd written, there was an unsettling tone in Grammy's voice. It
sounded like she was frightened, as if Aunt Ellen posed some
kind of threat. He was used to seeing her drunk, but tonight she
seemed more loaded than usual. Heart pounding in his chest, he

pulled his hand out of his backpack and crept to the door of his room, then down the hall.

The voices from the guest room grew louder, not just because he was getting closer to them but because Grammy and Ellen were now shouting. He barely had to lean in toward the door to catch each word.

"She was starting her 'don't have a baby' spee-eech. Jack heard every word." Ellen *tsked*. "Poor kid. Poor Jack. Wait until he finds...finds...out that Carrie's Romeo is my baby's daddy."

Wait a second. What?

"Ellen!" Michelle snapped, working to keep her voice down. "You said you wouldn't say anything. How does that mind of yours work? One second you say no one will ever know the truth, and the next, you're getting ready to share it with the world. What the hell is wrong with you? Have you no compassion?"

"None."

"Jesus, Ellen. First you blackmail Andrew by telling him you'll reveal his affair with a man and then you..."

She'll reveal his dad's what?

Jack stumbled back against the wall. The thud and the creak of the floorboards under his feet sounded as loud as the high school orchestra launching into the prologue as the curtain lifted. Heart pounding like a drum, he rushed back into his room. Even there he felt too exposed, too unprotected from everything going on around him. So he slid into his closet and hid between the hanging shirts that held the soothing scent of the fabric softener he loved so much. His mother used it occasionally for its softening properties until Jack told her there was something about its scent that calmed him. After that, she used it every time she washed his clothes. But right now, as he stood with metal hangers jabbing his back, not even fabric softener could quiet Jack's nerves. His insides were trembling... from the words he'd read in Aunt Ellen's journal and just heard coming from his grandmother's mouth.

Grammy's footsteps resonated through the quiet house as she headed down the hall, probably to investigate the sound he'd made. But there was another sound, too — muffled voices reached Jack's ears, coming rapidly and with a force that suggested if it weren't for the doors and coats between him and them, they'd be very loud. His parents were locked in their own argument. Jack remained frozen in the closet, listening with all he had even though he'd give anything to be spared the knowledge of what they were saying.

Grammy's steps paused as she listened, too. Their voices were still muffled, but Jack wasn't sure if it was because he was in his closet or their bedroom door helped curb the clarity of their words.

After a few more seconds, his grandmother backed up, her shadow cutting across the narrow space where he hadn't pulled his bedroom door all the way shut. Jack held his breath as she peeked inside. Nothing seemed to arouse her suspicions, and she continued down the hall. Soon he heard the door of the guest bedroom closing behind her.

Jack stayed in the closet, the heat of anger helping to stop his inner jitters. He didn't know which of his father's affairs to stress about first — the one he'd been having with a man for years and hiding from his family for just as long, or the one with his own wife's sister. And then there was Aunt Ellen, acting even more unhinged than usual. Had she found out about his dad's other lover and became jealous, sending her over the edge? Farther over the edge? And how was Mom going to handle it, being betrayed by both her husband and her sister?

But to be honest, Jack couldn't be surprised to learn another fucked-up thing Aunt Ellen did. He liked her, sometimes, but she was a mess. She'd probably done it just to hurt Mom. His father, though....the man he'd modeled his life after...he'd turned out to be a piece of *shit*.

Except Aunt Ellen's twisted actions *did* matter. Jack's legs gave out under him and he turned so he could slide to the floor of his closet. There didn't seem to be enough air in here and the thought of what Aunt Ellen's admission, confession, bullshit, whatever it was, made him feel as though he were about to suffocate. He quietly sneaked out of the closet and leaned against his dresser surrounded by the darkness of his bedroom. Ahhhh... now he could breathe. He inhaled deeply, twice, and let each breath out slowly.

The words between him and his mother from Aunt Ellen's last visit echoed inside his head: *"The three of us are like the three legs of a tripod that support each other. We stick together, no matter what,"* he'd said, to which she replied, *"Exactly! And I won't let anything or anyone damage that support."*

Well, Jack wasn't going to let anyone threaten the strength of their tripod.

Not even Aunt Ellen.

The woman had been a troublemaker, always saying and doing things that brought stress and tension into the house. It was as if she had only two goals in life: make her mother angry and get his parents to argue. But this pregnancy thing was different; this time she'd gone a step too far and it was up to him to make sure she didn't take another one. This had to be her final step. He couldn't allow her to open her big mouth and hurl stories, true or false, that would tear his family apart. He had to do something.

But what?

Before he could think up an answer, the guest room door creaked open and his aunt stumbled through it.

"I know what I do and d-don't need. What I need...what I need is something to help me forget what just came out of your mouth. Maybe I'll fi-find my journal down there too. Thanks to you, I now have a shitload to write."

Squinting in the dim light, he watched as she made it down the hall to the beginning of the staircase. There she went from leaning heavily against the wall to leaning on the banister, shaky as a leaf in a windstorm. She took two steps down, each one a precarious dance with gravity.

A surge of desperation washed over Jack, pulling him toward the staircase like a marionette on strings held by unseen hands.

Aunt Ellen paused, her head swiveling as if she'd heard a sound he'd been trying not to make. He froze, didn't even take a breath, as he waited for her to turn back around. One one thousand... two one thousand... three one thousand... four... Once she finally shifted her gaze back to the staircase and Jack felt confident her suspicions had faded, he crept up behind her with the stealth of a lion slithering toward its prey. As she attempted to descend another step, he reached out. His hand closed around her wrist above the banister. He yanked her hand away, leaving her teetering on the edge of the step.

His heart pounded in his chest, a wild drum playing the song of his fear. But he was in too deep. They both were... the fate of his family was now resting on his shoulders. He squeezed his eyes shut and shoved an open palm against Ellen's back.

The world seemed to slow as she tumbled down the stairs, the sickening sounds of her fall echoing in his ears. He raced down beside her, and then passed her, his stomach churning when he thought he heard something snap inside her body.

When he reached the bottom, he darted into the darkness of the kitchen, his hands shaking. He pulled open the refrigerator door so if anyone came in, he could pretend to be searching for a midnight snack. The cold air breathed over his flushed face.

Suddenly, the hallway and staircase were bathed in light. He bolted toward them, only to skid to a halt above Aunt Ellen. He kneeled beside her body. Her eyes stared blankly at the ceiling. With a trembling hand he reached out to touch her shoulder.

He glanced up the stairs to see his parents and grandmother at the top, their faces wide-eyed masks of shock. They turned away from him and Ellen to look at one another accusingly. He was stunned they weren't running down the steps to check on Ellen's condition. What is wrong with them? They seemed more consumed with how it happened than the life, or death, of the woman at the foot of the stairs. *What in the holy fuck?*

He looked back down at his aunt, his heart getting heavy with the weight of his actions. He closed his eyes, steeling himself for the performance of a lifetime.

Then he looked up toward the figures at the top of the stairs.

"Why aren't you doing anything?" he screamed. "Get down here! Call 9-1-1!"

Andrew slid his phone from his pants pocket and tapped the screen once, then three times. Carrie and Michelle exchanged a glance, a silent communication that spoke volumes, before they rushed down the stairs to join Jack. He was now stroking the top of her head with his hand.

Carrie felt Ellen's wrist for a pulse while Michelle tenderly brushed the hair from her daughter's forehead. Their eyes met over Ellen's motionless body and they both held an expression that told Jack she was dead.

Jack bent down and pressed his ear to Ellen's mouth. "She's not breathing," he said, blinking tears out of his eyes to fall onto her neck.

"I have to try CPR!" He almost choked on the words, and it wasn't all a performance. "I learned it in school last year." He moved to turn her over, but his mom stopped him with a hand on his back.

"Jack, don't move her. Look at her neck." She pointed to grotesque bulges and an angry, swollen mound of discolored skin. Ellen's neck was twisted at an angle that reminded him of his next-door neighbor's doll whose head had once been yanked off and improperly reattached.

"She's gone," Carrie whispered.

Jack remained on his knees, but he lifted his eyes from Ellen's lifeless body to his mother, his grandmother, and then his father, still at the top of the stairs. The audience at *West Side Story* had been a sea of tears and sniffles. This audience was different. Their faces were a jumble of emotions — shock, fear, and a strange, but detached sadness. From the lack of tears or words of distress or sorrow, Jack saw their tangled expressions were not for the woman lying dead at the foot of the stairs, but for the circumstances that had led to this moment.

"Hello? Earth to Jack." Donna waved a hand in front of his face.

He met her gaze, smiling sheepishly. "Yeah, sorry about that. I was just...lost in thought. So, what's this film called?"

Donna's eyes sparkled with a hint of excitement as she

leaned forward, her hands clasped tightly, as if holding onto a secret she was told not to share. *"The Final Step."*

Jack let the title sink in, rolling it around in his mind like a fine wine. It was ominous, intriguing, and based on his own life story, entirely appropriate. He looked at Donna, his smile widening into a full-blown grin.

"Sounds perfect," he said. "When do I start?"

If you enjoyed "The Final Step",

please take a moment to share it with others

by leaving a review on Amazon or Goodreads.

Other books by Rob Kaufman

Standalone Books

One Last Lie

A Broken Reality

The Perfect Ending

In the Shadow of Stone

Justin Wright Suspense Series

Altered

Jaded

Avenged

Scared

(coming January 2024)

ABOUT THE AUTHOR

Rob's success in the psychological thriller genre can be attributed to his unique combination of a psychology degree and storytelling skills.

With his deep understanding of human behavior and the intricacies of the human mind, Rob creates characters that readers can relate to on a personal level. He taps into universal emotions, fears, and desires, crafting complex and multi-dimensional characters that resonate with the readers.

One of Rob's strengths lies in his ability to take his readers on a captivating journey filled with suspense and tension. From the very beginning of his books, he hooks the readers with intriguing and enigmatic openings, leaving them yearning for more.

Rob masterfully weaves intricate plots, full of twists and turns, keeping the readers guessing and on the edge of their seats throughout the entire story. He skillfully builds suspense, gradually revealing clues and secrets, leading to a climax that often surpasses the readers' expectations.

Made in the USA
Columbia, SC
28 December 2023

48aaec88-76a0-4df6-b9b8-cb46b6b0bf1eR01